PETER JOINS IN

Peter Mason is bitter, unhappy and had a bad reputation in the village. Alan, his friend goes to see Richard Harding about helping Peter. It is Richard who teaches Peter about Christianity and encouarages him to join in and make friends. Alan's friendship with Peter becomes strained and Peter's life at home continues to be difficult, but in the end Peter comes to a memorable decision.

GATEWAY BOOKS

Belle's Bridle
Beryl Bye

The Black Pirate
James Cahill

Butterfly Summer
Christine Wood

Change With Me
Chris Savery

The Far-Farers
Chris Savery

Fisherman Jack
Mary St Helier

Friends for Joanna
Elisabeth Batt

Jamaican Schoolgirl
Elisabeth Batt

Joan's Crusade
Eileen Heming

Johnny Next Door
N.W. Hanssen

Marion's Venture
Dorothy Marsh

Nobody's Pony
Beryl Bye

Nurse Millaray
Dorothy Royce

Oak House
Susan Trought

One Too Many
Peggie C. Moody

The Open Door
Eileen Heming

Pat's New Life
Dorothy Marsh

Peter Joins In
L.V. Davidson

Pony for Sale
Beryl Bye

Ruth the Rebel
L.V. Davidson

The Secret of
Woodside Cottage
L.V. Davidson

Siege of Blackbrae
Chris Savery

Summer at End House
Diana Green

Young Elizabeth Green
Constance Savery

PETER JOINS IN

L. V. DAVIDSON

LUTTERWORTH PRESS
CAMBRIDGE

Lutterworth Press
P.O. Box 60
Cambridge CB1 2NT

British Library Cataloguing in Publication Data available

The verses of the hymn on page 119 are reprinted from *Sankey's Sacred Songs and Solos*, by kind permission of the publishers, Messrs. Marshall, Morgan and Scott.

ISBN 0 7188 1947 0

First published 1955 by Lutterworth Press
First paperback edition 1972
Reprinted 1978, 1988

Printed by
The Guernsey Press Co. Ltd., Guernsey, Channel Islands.

CONTENTS

Chapter 1

THE PROBLEM OF PETER

A DELICIOUS smell of baking pervaded the farmhouse kitchen, as Mrs. Ferguson turned from the oven and deposited a large tray of scones on the table, just as her son, Alan, pushed open the door and sniffed appreciatively.

"Hullo, Mum! I'm starving!" he announced, at the same time picking up a scone and as quickly dropping it again.

Mrs. Ferguson gave his hand a playful slap as now, holding the hot scone in an unspeakably dirty handkerchief, he began cautiously nibbling round its edge. "Don't spoil your appetite for tea," she warned, "we'll have it in half an hour, and put that horrible hanky to the wash."

"A few scones won't make any difference to *my* tea," Alan answered placidly, helping himself to another.

His mother hastily picked up the tray, and carried it away with an indulgent laugh.

"Why are you so late home from school?" The question was catapulted across the room from a girl who, curled up on the end of the old sofa and apparently absorbed in a book, had up to now not appeared to notice her brother's entrance.

"I'm not late, and it's no business of yours, anyhow," the boy replied carelessly.

Ella's eyes flashed. "That's just where you're wrong," she declared, hotly. "You've been with that wretched boy again. Why you've got to choose a creature like that for a friend, I don't know. There are plenty of decent boys about. It's certainly my business when everyone is talking about us."

Alan's fair face had turned scarlet with anger. He was beginning an indignant retort when his mother, who had come back into the room and was in the act of spreading the cloth on the table in preparation for tea, intervened.

"What is the matter?" she demanded. "Whom are you talking about?"

"Only that Alan is always with that dreadful boy, Peter Mason, and people are beginning to think him as bad as he is," Ella said with a contemptuous sniff. She was nearly sixteen, five years older than her brother, and at an age when "what people thought" seemed of very great importance indeed.

Mrs. Ferguson looked troubled. She turned to her son, whose usually cheerful, open face now wore a decided scowl.

"I hope this isn't true, Alan," she said gravely. "I wouldn't like you to make a friend of that boy, he has a dreadful name in the village."

"It's not his fault," Alan defended, "he's all right really. Just because he's poor and hasn't any real people of his own, people are beastly to him."

"Nonsense, Alan," Mrs. Ferguson spoke with unwonted sharpness, "the boy's been in trouble with the police more than once. He's dirty and wild, and uses bad language. You're not to have anything to do with him."

Alan's face took on an even deeper shade of crimson; a most surprising and embarrassing lump rose in his throat; he turned away without answering, and, with hunched shoulders and hands thrust deep in his pockets, went out of the room.

His mother's eyes followed him with a troubled expression; then she turned to her daughter. "How long has this been going on, do you suppose?" she asked.

Ella shrugged her shoulders. "Quite a while, but they're getting thicker all the time and are always together."

"You might have spoken about it before, then, and with a little more tact. Father will be furious if he thinks Alan's making a friend of that disreputable boy, and it would have been much easier checked in the beginning. Come along and lay the table," she added as she turned away.

Ella put down her book with a reluctant sigh; she was an inveterate reader and not at all fond of domestic duties of any kind.

Upstairs, in the tiny slip of a room over the front door, Alan was staring out on the grey February landscape. He had come trudging up the narrow footway at the edge of the ploughed field with such a warm, happy glow in his heart; the solemn compact of friendship which he and Peter Mason had undertaken had seemed to him such a fine and satisfying thing. They had vowed to stick to each other through thick and thin, and to allow nothing to come between them. His mind had been full of plans as he had faced the biting wind that swept down that last steep field. He would take his mother into his confidence at the earliest opportunity, get her to invite Peter to tea; the poor chap never knew what it was to have a decent meal. Mother, too, might find some way of helping him to look less forlorn and unkempt in his appearance, do something, perhaps, about the torn jacket and hopelessly short trousers, at which some of the boys had laughed so cruelly to-day. Alan had great faith in his mother and knew her kind heart; but now everything was spoilt; for the moment he felt he hated his sister. Never in his life had he been in such a dilemma. To break his promises to Peter as soon as they had been made seemed unthinkable, yet deliberate and persistent disobedience to his parents he had never before contemplated for a moment. Alan clenched his hands hard and felt the unwelcome prick of actual tears behind his eyes.

The tea-bell was not the welcome sound it usually was to his ears, indeed, for a moment or two, he hesitated about going down at all; but decided that to remain away would have the inevitable effect of dragging his father into the unhappy business, and this he still hoped might somehow be avoided.

Mr. Ferguson was a busy and practical farmer. He was very fond and proud of his children, especially Ella, who had won a scholarship for High School, and went by bus or bicycle every day to the nearest town. He was a great believer in education and was willing to make any necessary effort to help her fulfil her ambition to have a University career; but he had left their general upbringing very largely to his wife, and seldom interfered with their plans in any way, always, however, upholding her authority if any serious question arose. Very much respected in the neighbourhood and acting as Vicar's Warden at the village church, he was an upright and proud man, and Alan knew only too well that his views on any friendly intimacy with poor Peter Mason would be even stronger than those of his wife.

As for Peter himself, he went home with a lighter step and more upright carriage than for many a long day. He swung open the little warped wooden gate, that hung dejectedly on one hinge, with almost a jaunty air, and passed along the path by the neglected untidy little bit of garden without the habitual scowl gathering on his brow. The door he opened led straight into a small close living-room; the lattice window might be considered picturesque, but let in very little light, and at the close of a dull February day the place appeared to be in semi-darkness. The stone floor was uncovered, save for a threadbare old mat before the hearth. A tall, angular woman was seated in a wooden-armed Windsor chair by the fire. Red, long hands rested on the coarse apron which covered her lap; greying hair was dragged tightly back into an unbecoming knob at the back of her head. She was not occupied in any way, but did not even raise her eyes at the boy's entrance. There was some rather soiled newspaper on the table which stood under the window, and on this a brown teapot, with a very chipped spout, a small end of a loaf and a piece of margarine partly wrapped in its original paper, were placed in close proximity to the unlighted oil-lamp.

The habitual scowl was beginning to gather again on Peter's brow. He went up to the table and felt the lukewarm teapot, then glanced at the kettle in the grate.

"I'd like some hot tea," he stated gruffly.

The woman turned a pair of pale blue eyes upon him, regarding him in a cold stony silence for some seconds which made him squirm uneasily. Then she spoke.

"So his lordship would like some hot tea. Better ring the bell for the butler to bring it, and the footman to fetch whatever else he may require."

It was not the cheap sarcasm of the words themselves which cut and stung, but the hard, bitter antagonism which was conveyed in the tone in which they were uttered. There was a dull flush on Peter's face as he turned back to the table, and savagely hacked at the remains of the loaf.

His aunt watched him for a moment, then continued, "Fresh tea, indeed! Tea costs nothing, I suppose. You can come in whenever you choose, and demand fresh tea. You ought to be thankful I didn't wash out the pot and put it away long ago. School's over an hour or more, so you needn't bother to tell me any lies—I know you've been up to no good since. Coming in as bold as brass and demanding fresh tea!" Once started, it seemed that Miss Mason was unable to stop. She kept up a continuous flow of complaint while the boy went on steadily munching the unappetizing bread and margarine with obvious hunger; nor did he move from the table till the last crumb had vanished. He had answered no word to the fault-finding and accusations, to which indeed he had appeared oblivious; now, though obviously far from satisfied, he rose, picked up his scarf—he had no overcoat—and after casting rather a wistful look at the fire, turned again to the door.

"Where are you going?" his aunt demanded sharply.

A contemptuous and very unchildlike smile played about Peter's mouth for a moment. "Wouldn't you like to know?" he asked scathingly. "You wouldn't believe me if I told you. Well, how about this? I'm going to blow a safe and rob the bank!" With that he pressed down the latch, passed through the narrow door, and banged it defiantly behind him.

The chill wind struck him full in the face as he turned down the village street; his threadbare clothes seemed to offer no protection whatever, and he shivered, and thrust his cold hands further down in his pockets, as he trudged drearily on, his mind, as usual, full of bitter, resentful thoughts. As he had told Alan that very day, he considered life a wash-out, not worth living, a system so unfair and unequal that one could only grab what one could for oneself without consideration for anybody else, and yet the very fact that he could express his thoughts to someone who met him on equal terms had somehow helped him. His ever-growing friendship with Alan Ferguson had been the central thing in his life for the past few weeks, and to-day the pledges they had made to each other had brought him an altogether new sense of warmth, comfort, and something like stability. He knew that Alan, with his comfortable home, affectionate parents, and assured prospects, could not really understand quite how utterly lonely and friendless he was; his pride would never let him disclose the full depths of the daily degradation of his lot, but it had been something at least to confide the bare outlines of his personal history. His mother had died when he was three years old, and his father, already a victim of tuberculosis, had come to live with his sister in the little cottage which Peter had just left. He too had died two years later, and Miss Mason had been left the sole protector of her small nephew. From the very first she had bitterly resented the task; never for a day was the child allowed to forget that he was a burden on his aunt's slender resources. As he grew older, recriminations and bitter words were almost the only mode of speech passing between them. Peter put in the minimum of time under the thatched roof that was the only home he knew. Neglected, unloved, and always hungry, he could hardly fail to get into mischief during the many hours he wandered about alone, especially during school holidays, and soon acquired an extremely bad name among neighbours; and even more so with farmers whose orchards and fruit gardens were never safe from him; he had even been accused of raiding a hen-house on some occasions, and carrying off new-laid eggs. He had more than once been in the hands of the village policeman for wanton and destructive stone-throwing and trespassing, and could not much longer hope to escape an official prosecution, the village gossips declared, with many a shake of the head. The majority were of the opinion that it would, on the whole, be a good thing if this should happen speedily and the boy placed in an approved school without further delay. Peter himself listened to warnings and reproofs with the same outward appearance of hardened indifference that he showed to the most violent tirades of his aunt; these he met with fairly frequently, when she had been made the recipient of stories of some of the more daring and outrageous of his misdemeanours. Beyond a sudden cuff, or box on the ear, Miss Mason had for some time given up all attempt at physical correction; at twelve years old Peter was as strong as she, and fiercely resisted any attempt of the kind. Though usually silent under her nagging tongue, he had at times a violent and ungovernable temper, before which, when fully roused, even his aunt quailed, and shuddered at the torrent of bad language which he could on occasion pour out. Such was Peter Mason, and it could hardly be wondered at that Mrs. Ferguson's heart sank at any idea of friendship between him and her cherished son.

The two boys had first become attracted to each other some three months earlier, when Alan had picked up a young owl with a broken wing. He was keenly interested in all living creatures, and was carrying it home, wrapped in his jacket to protect himself from its pecks, when he had met Peter, who had shown himself remarkably skilful and tender in dealing with the unfortunate bird's injury. They had housed the patient in an outhouse on the Fergusons' farm and, though in spite of every care it only survived three days, their mutual interest and efforts had drawn them together. Intermittently at first, but of late very steadily, the friendship had grown, reaching what seemed to both boys a climax that afternoon, when for the first time Peter had opened up a little on the subject of his past life and present trials. Warm-hearted Alan was deeply stirred, and it was he who had suggested the compact of friendship, when each boy had solemnly vowed to be a loyal friend to the other, no matter in what circumstances or conditions they found themselves.

Without any conscious plan as to the direction he should take, Peter found himself, drawn by the memory of that heart-warming promise, walking up the same ploughed field that Alan had climbed earlier in the evening. He could not have said why he chose this way, as there was little hope of seeing his friend, and he certainly had no intention of making his presence known to the Ferguson family. It was very dark, except for brief intervals when the strong wind blew the clouds from the face of the moon, but presently the farm buildings loomed up before him, and, crossing the yard, he cautiously approached the house. Light was shining out with a cheery glow through the red curtains of the big kitchen window; they were not closely drawn, and by putting his eye to the space of about three inches where they did not meet he could see a good part of the room: the back of Farmer Ferguson's head as he sat, with feet stretched out to the fire, absorbed in his paper; Mrs. Ferguson on the opposite side with hand in a sock, plying a big needle; Ella at the table which was piled with books, evidently busy with homework; and Alan slouched low in a chair, hands in pockets. One look at Alan was sufficient to show that something had gone seriously wrong with that usually lighthearted and merry individual, but in spite of this fact, the scene looked so essentially peaceful and homelike, and above all warm, that a profound sigh coming up from somewhere at the very depth of his being shook the watcher at the window, while another icy blast of wind cut through the threadbare jacket and set his teeth chattering. If only he could attract Alan's attention, but to do so without disturbing the rest of the family was manifestly impossible, and after another prolonged and hungry stare he reluctantly turned away. A dog barked fiercely as he made his way across the yard with some idea of seeking shelter in an outhouse or barn. If he could only get into the cowshed he could get some warmth from the animals' bodies, but, alas, it was securely fastened, and the dog was now barking with such violence that he heard the back door open, caught a fleeting vision of Mr. Ferguson's burly form framed in the lighted entrance, and fled. The farmer heard the running feet and shouted, then hastened to unchain the dog, who was soon in hot pursuit. Peter was now in the field; he had no fear of dogs and stood quite still in the shelter of the hedge as soon as this one was near enough to hail softly.

"Hi, Scout, good fellow!" he called, holding out his hand; he could see the gleaming eyes in the darkness, but not the gradual subsiding of the bristling hair. The next moment a cold nose touched his hand. "Good old Scout. You didn't really think you were going to bite me, did you?" he said, patting the dog's head. "Now, let me go quickly."

The farmer had gone back for a torch and was now taking a hurried look round the yard, where, however, all seemed to be in order.

Keeping well in to the hedge, Peter made what speed he could in the darkness, breaking into a run as soon as he reached the road. The cottage was in darkness when he arrived, breathless, but decidedly warmer than when he started. The door, however, was seldom bolted and he stepped into the comparative warmth of the kitchen, felt about for the matches, and cautiously lighted an end of candle on which long practice enabled him to lay his hand in the dark without difficulty. His glance went swiftly to the grate, but the fire was out; only a tiny glow showing here and there among the grey ashes as he eagerly raked them over. It was only nine o'clock, but Miss

Mason frequently went to bed at a very early hour to save fire and light; also, as Peter firmly believed, to deny him the comfort of the warmth. He had no doubt that she was listening intently to his movements now, and he untied and removed his boots before creeping noiselessly across the floor to open the door of the tiny lean-to which served as scullery and store cupboard at the back. There was little choice in the way of eatables; a packet of porridge oats, a small uncut loaf, half a pot of marmalade, the margarine he had left uneaten in the evening, and a jug of milk. Nevertheless, the boy's eyes gleamed with a mixture of hunger and mischief. He cut a thick crust from one end of the loaf and spread it generously with marmalade, then he picked up the jug of milk, put it down again and hesitated; finally he carried it back with him to the hearth and, getting as close to the dead fire as he could, devoured his crust and drained the milk jug. There would be no milk for the tea in the morning, and what a row there would be! He shrugged his shoulders. "She" had refused him a cup of hot tea earlier, and that hers should be spoilt in retaliation seemed to him no more than justice. He placed the jug back exactly where he had found it, closed the marmalade pot, and wiped the knife clean in the damp dish-cloth, then stole silently upstairs to the smaller of the two tiny bedrooms the cottage contained.

Chapter 2

WOODSIDE COTTAGE AGAIN

THOUGH she appeared absorbed in her sock-mending, Mrs. Ferguson was unobtrusively watching her boy uneasily. His obvious depression was so unusual that even Mr. Ferguson glanced at him over his paper several times, and Ella found the unaccustomed peace and quiet she was getting for her homework much less pleasant than she would have cared to confess. Scout's furious barking came as almost a welcome relief. Mr. Ferguson came back after a second inspection of the premises with the aid of his torch with the news that someone had certainly been about and up to no good, he had heard running feet distinctly and the dog had given chase but returned in a remarkably short time. Though some conversation on tramps, burglars, and chicken-stealers followed, Alan took little part in it, and when a short time later his mother suggested that it was his bedtime, he astonished the rest of the family by immediate acquiescence instead of the usual protests and pleadings for at least another half-hour.

"What's the matter with the boy?" the farmer asked, with raised eyebrows.

"A bit overtired and out of sorts, I think," his wife answered hastily, and gave Ella a warning look as soon as the paper was raised again.

When she thought Alan would be ready, she went upstairs and sat down on her son's bed, with the invitation, "Tell me what's upsetting you so much."

The story, at least part of it, poured out with all the eloquence of which Alan was capable. The fine points in Peter's character, his friendless, unhappy circumstances, how he himself had depended on his mother's kindness and understanding to help, and, finally, the promise which, he declared, it was quite impossible for him to break.

Mrs. Ferguson listened to it all with mounting concern. She did not know much of village affairs, as the farm was well outside. As Churchwarden's wife, she usually went to church once on Sunday, belonged to but did not regularly attend the Women's Institute, was friendly with all her neighbours, but had no very intimate friends. Of Miss Mason, who came neither to church nor to the Institute, she knew nothing personally, and was inclined to think that Peter had grossly exaggerated her attitude towards him, and her estimation of his character was not improved by what she considered the disloyalty and ingratitude of talking about his aunt behind her back. Nevertheless, Alan's wholehearted faith in his friend, his eloquent pleading and evident deep concern and trouble were not without their effect on a mother who found it very hard to deny her only son anything. Provided no walks or excursions were undertaken together, she would not forbid Alan to speak to Peter at school, at least until she had made some further inquiries into the real state of affairs in the Mason household, though this she was secretly very reluctant to do, being a firm believer in minding one's own business on all occasions. She had the satisfaction, however, of leaving the boy decidedly happier when she finally tucked him up and returned to the kitchen.

Her husband was out having a final look round and Ella looked up with "What an age you've been, Mother."

"I've been talking to Alan about that boy. Don't mention the trouble to your father, I'll settle this myself," Mrs. Ferguson replied, as she began straightening the room and making preparation for the next morning's work.

Alan had no opportunity of speaking to his friend till the mid-morning break at school next day, when Peter showed a strong inclination to hug the schoolroom stove instead of dashing out to the playground as soon as the bell sounded, only going sulkily forth when ordered out by the master. It took Alan some time to coax the reason of his gloom out of him, but, after a little, a glint of mischief showed in his eyes and he explained that there had been a first-class row at home that morning, when his aunt had discovered his raid on their larder the previous evening, as a result of which she had refused him food of any kind before he came to school, even calling after him that he need not return to dinner either. Alan's heart swelled with indignation as he listened; silently he passed the large piece of cake he had brought for his own lunch to his friend.

Peter eyed it hungrily, then he said gruffly, "Shares."

"Don't be an ass, I don't want it. Go on. What were you doing out last night?" Alan urged.

"Up at your place. I saw you." Peter grinned as he took a huge, delicious bite, and warmed to his story as the other listened round-eyed.

Something of the pathos of his chosen friend being out in the cold, dismal, winter night, while he sat well-fed and protected by a bright fire, gripped Alan's warm heart and quick imagination. For a moment or two he could hardly speak. If only he could make his mother really understand and believe Peter's need!

"Aren't you going home for dinner, really?" he asked presently.

"Not much, I'm not." Peter's lip curled, scornfully. "Do you think I'm going begging round her?"

Alan was appalled, yet his own pride made him applaud his friend's resolution. "You just can't go on starving, all the same!" he urged. "Try to stick it till I come back and I'll bring you grub of some sort."

"Won't your mother kick up a shindy?" Peter asked doubtfully.

"No, she'll let me have it all right," Alan answered with more assurance than he really felt, though he made an inward resolution not to return to afternoon school without food of some sort, no matter what means he had to employ to obtain it.

He ran the greater part of the way home in his anxiety to get his mother to himself for a few minutes before his father came in. Ella had dinner at school, so Mrs. Ferguson was the only occupant of the kitchen when he burst breathlessly in, and threw himself upon her in a boisterous hug.

"Mum, you wouldn't let anyone starve to death even if you hated them, would you?" he demanded.

"Whatever are you talking about? Of course I wouldn't!" his mother answered. "What's the matter with you, puffing like a grampus? Who's starving?"

She went on dishing up the hot appetizing dinner as Alan told his story, only omitting the fact that Peter had been their mysterious visitor of the previous night. She shook her head and clicked her tongue several times during the recital.

"Well," she said, when Alan at length paused for breath, "if all this is true, which I very much doubt, it's certainly wrong of Miss Mason to send a child out to school without food, though if she did, I've no doubt that Peter had tried her past bearing. I don't for a minute suppose she meant it about not giving him any dinner."

"She *did* mean it," Alan affirmed. "Peter said if he went home she would have had hers early and there wouldn't be a scrap of anything. It's happened before. If you saw him, you'd know it was all true. He looked awful by break-time to-day. Mum, I simply can't eat my dinner if you won't let me take something to Peter."

Mrs. Ferguson again clicked her tongue disapprovingly but yielded. "Very well, Alan. I don't want the boy to be hungry on such a cold day, but don't think you can make a practice of carrying out food to him, it's only encouraging him to defy his aunt. Now go to the back door and ring the bell for your father."

"You're a good sport, Mum." Alan gave her another boisterous hug, then went and plied the large handbell with extreme vigour. When he came back he noticed that two eggs were already boiling at the side of the stove and guessed rightly that they were destined for Peter. Later these hard-boiled eggs, and a generous pile of thick ham sandwiches, did much to restore his friend to a more optimistic outlook on life.

Mrs. Ferguson, however, was far from satisfied with the course of events, and anxiously turned over in her mind what action she ought to take. She very seldom went into the village, being fully occupied with home duties, and was quite at a loss as to whom she could consult on so delicate a matter; her face grew hot at the mere thought of being accused of interference in her neighbour's business. The Vicar's wife was not very active in the parish, and as Miss Mason was not even a churchgoer, was quite unlikely to prove helpful. There was young Mrs. Stanhope, the solicitor's wife, who lived at the Manor House; she had heard that she visited among the cottages, but the thought of approaching her was a severe ordeal, and she sighed heavily and turned to her afternoon's work in a mood far removed from her usual cheerful energy.

The next day was Saturday. There had been hard frost in the night, and having accomplished a number of small chores which were always expected of him on that day, Alan was eager to rush off to see if the ice on the village pond would bear for sliding.

"Mind you don't go on if it's not safe," his mother cautioned in the manner of mothers from time immemorial. "There's no fun in getting soaked to your skin and ruining your clothes, and," she added, "I want you to leave these eggs at Woodside Cottage as you pass."

Alan's face fell; the errand was an unwelcome one; he could not make half the speed he had anticipated if he had to carry eggs. He accepted the bag without grumbling, however, and set off as fast as he dared. Woodside Cottage was the last house in the village, and he passed it every day on his journeys to and from school. Once or twice before he had handed in eggs to the nurse-housekeeper who looked after the invalid gentleman who had lived there for the past four years. He was a man still in his early thirties who, had been a pilot. He had had a serious illness and for sometime had been completely paralysed from the waist down.

Woodside Cottage was a long, low house, running at right angles to the road. As he stood at the unlatched front door the boy could see the cheerful play of firelight reflected from the windows on his left. His knock was answered by a man's voice calling, "Come in." Rather shyly Alan crossed the threshold and stood hesitatingly in the small flagged hall.

"In here, please," the voice called again, and the boy opened the door of the room from which he had noticed the fire, and looked shyly round him. He saw at once that it was a most interesting room, but dared not let his eyes wander more than a moment to the wonderful little model planes and carved ivories with which it abounded.

The man who had called him was lying on a sofa drawn up a little distance from the bright fire; his legs were covered with a rug, but his face still showed scars, and his mouth was drawn to one side in a most peculiar manner. He smiled at the boy, however, without self-consciousness.

"Do come right in. I'm all alone for just a few minutes," he began. "My housekeeper found she was out of one of the many mysteries that she considers necessary for cooking, and has gone to the shop. May I know your name?"

"I'm Alan Ferguson." Alan drew a deep breath. "My mother sent some eggs. Shall I put them down here?"

"Thank you very much indeed. Yes, please do, and then come and sit down if you can spare a few minutes, it's so jolly for me to have an unexpected visitor."

The boy came forward slowly, his feelings a mixture of impatience and curiosity. He wanted to be off to the pond, but was nevertheless interested in his host, to whom from time to time he had heard somewhat conflicting allusions in the village. Some referred to him almost with bated breath as a hero and a saint; others with dubious sniffs called him a crank and a fanatic, whatever that might mean. He had heard his facial disfigurement described with horror and revulsion, and again passed by as of no account whatever. He forced himself to take a good look now, and came to the conclusion that after the first shock it did not really detract from the steady kindliness and strength which shone from the eyes. One or two questions about himself and school set Alan's tongue wagging, then came the startling one, "Have you a very special pal?"

The boy stared in silence for a moment and Richard Harding raised his eyebrows. "I see, there is something particular about that subject, so if I shouldn't have asked, don't answer, and let's forget it," he said quickly.

"It seemed almost as if you knew." Alan hesitated. He was the more surprised of the two when he found himself, after a brief interval, actually telling this stranger his difficulties about Peter Mason. He was talking hard when Miss Cooper, the housekeeper, came back, looked in at the door to receive a smile and cheerful wave of the hand from Mr. Harding, and withdrew to the kitchen.

She returned presently with a tray containing two steaming cups of coffee and a plate of biscuits. Alan jumped up in some embarrassment, declaring that he must go, but Mr. Harding pointed out that it would be a shame not to drink the coffee now that it was poured out, and once they were alone again the story went on.

"There is bound to be a way to help Peter," the invalid said with such assurance that Alan felt his own confidence being given an immense lift, and waited eagerly for the next words. These astonished him so much that for a moment he could only stare open-mouthed at his host, while he grew scarlet to the roots of his hair.

"I must talk to my Commander about it," Richard Harding said, in the most ordinary and natural manner. "Without His direction, any scheme we may think up will come to nothing." Then, smiling at the boy's puzzled face, he added, "Only the Lord Jesus Christ can be of any permanent help to Peter. I thought perhaps you knew Him too, and that was why you cared so much about it."

It was then that Alan blushed and, for the first time since he had entered the room, heartily wished that he had not come.

His new friend watched him a moment, then said cheerfully, "Don't let my blundering words upset you, Alan. It would have been grand to know that you and I were in the same Royal Service in this matter and in everything else, but just now we've got to decide on the first step to be taken on Peter's behalf, and, as I told you, I must ask about that or I'm bound to make a mistake."

Alan longed to ask how this strange man expected to receive an answer, but the overwhelming embarrassment which came over him whenever what he called "religious subjects" were mentioned held him silent. "I'd better be going," he said again uneasily, once more getting to his feet, "thanks a lot."

"Very well." Mr. Harding held out his hand. "Thank *you* for keeping me company so long, but when can you come back to discuss things? Once we know where the start is to be made, I shan't be able actually to *do* anything at all without you, you see."

Once more Alan's hopes, which had received a severe setback, began to rise; apparently this strange man did really mean business after all.

"I can come whenever you like," he promised.

"Good, well, how about tea-time to-day, say four o'clock? The sooner we get going, the better." The tone was so enthusiastic that the boy was still further encouraged to believe that something really might come of these very odd methods of approaching the problem; still he did most heartily wish that religion had not been brought into it. Mr. Harding certainly introduced it in a more natural and realistic way than Alan had ever heard before, but it would be fatal to attempt to touch Peter by any such means, he was quite sure. He had been shocked at the language his pal had used in expressing his utter disdain of the whole crowd of those who professed religion in any form, whom he dubbed humbugs and hypocrites.

It was after twelve o'clock and he should be in to dinner at half-past, but even at the risk of being very late, he decided to make a dash for it and see if he could find Peter. He could hear the shouts of the other boys before he rounded the bend in the road which brought him in view of the large pond, which seemed to have attracted nearly all the boys of the village that morning. The ice was bearing well at one end, and a well-marked slide stretched across it from bank to bank, over which a continuous string of boys were passing, racing round as soon as they reached one side to join on at the back of those starting from the other. Alan was hailed with a few cheery shouts and could not resist joining the fun for just one or two swift glides over the ice, but all the time his eyes were busy searching for his friend.

"Have you seen Peter Mason?" he asked the boy just in front of him, as he lined up for his second turn.

The other shook his head, then remembered. "He was here when I first came, for a bit, but what do you want him for? He's no good. My father says I'm not to have anything to do with him."

Alan did not answer. He took his slide, then left the line and started for home, his face grave. Poor Peter, what a shame it was; everyone was against him. He wondered if he had left the sport at the pond because he had been deliberately cold-shouldered. There did not seem much hope of a helpless invalid being able to do anything to improve matters when all the active members of the village appeared so determined to hang the dog with the bad name. Alan kicked a stone angrily; he was furious with himself for spending so much of the morning talking to Mr. Harding when he might have prevented Peter from feeling himself such an outcast from society. It was this feeling of not being wanted anywhere which was embittering the lad, and making him grow more surly and uncouth in his manners day by day.

Dinner was more than half-way through when he got home, and he had to endure a sharp reproof from his father, though his mother set the well-filled plate she had kept steaming hot before him without comment. He and Ella were expected to do the washing up on Saturdays, while Mrs. Ferguson made ready to go on her weekly shopping expedition. They got on well enough as a rule with a good deal of sparring and laughter, but to-day both seemed somewhat preoccupied. Alan was thinking of the visit he was to pay that afternoon, and wondering what possible good could come of it, even though he had found himself personally greatly attracted to his host, but after a while his sister's unusual silence struck him as odd and he gave her a sudden poke as he said ironically, "Don't talk so much."

Ella frowned, and scraped at the saucepan she was cleaning, without retaliation. This was so surprising that the boy's attention was caught.

"What's up?" he asked, in quite a different tone.

His sister sighed. "You wouldn't understand, but I'm so worried I'll tell you," she answered surprisingly, "only don't go chattering about it. Dad wants me to be confirmed. The Vicar is starting classes, you know. I put it off last time they asked me, but now it's difficult."

Alan stared perplexedly. "Why?" he asked. "What difference does it make?"

Ella gave a short laugh. "That's just it," she said, "it doesn't make a scrap of difference, but it ought to, and I hate being a hypocrite and a perjurer."

"A what?" Alan asked in bewilderment.

"A perjurer. That's somebody who swears falsely."

Her brother gave a low whistle. "You don't

have to swear anything, do you?" he asked in rather awestruck tones. "I thought you just dressed up like a bride and the Bishop came and put his hand on your head."

"That's just about what it amounts to with most people," his sister agreed, "but you do have to take a sort of vow, and when you don't mean to keep it I think it's a rotten thing to do."

Alan was intrigued. "What do you vow?" he asked with interest.

Ella slapped the dishcloth on to its hook impatiently. "It's quite a lot, all the things people are supposed to promise for a baby when it's christened. That's what being confirmed means, that you take all those promises on yourself. It means at least that you undertake to be a Christian. Look at all the wiping-up you've still got," she added sharply.

Alan had been standing idle, cloth in hand, for the last few minutes; now he picked up a vegetable dish and began to wipe it slowly round.

"Half a mo!" he exclaimed as Ella turned away, "aren't we Christians anyhow?"

The girl shrugged her shoulders, her lip curled a little. "We're just cheap imitations," she answered, "the real thing is quite different."

She left him then, though Alan called after her, "A real Christian would help finish all this beastly wiping-up!" The hint had no effect and he turned to his task still feeling puzzled. "What a queer thing that religion should keep on coming up like this to-day," he mused. "I'd never have dreamt Ella gave it a thought. I wonder if she'll have the guts not to be confirmed."

It was beginning to thaw, he could hear the slow drip of water from the overhanging eaves as he went back to the warm, bright kitchen. He helped himself to an apple *en route* and sat down by the fire to enjoy it, yet with an uneasy wonder as to how Peter was spending the day. Idle Saturdays with nowhere to go and nothing to do were a ripe source of mischief and trouble. He wished now that he had told his mother about the invitation to Woodside Cottage, for though he expected to be back in time for the family tea at half-past five, it had suddenly dawned on him that he ought to put on his best suit for such an occasion. But to take it without her approval would be an unheard-of action in the Ferguson household. He had to content himself with changing from his old Saturday clothes into the more respectable school ones, combing his hair with a very wet comb, and giving his shoes a rather perfunctory brush. There was no one about at all when he left the house at 3.45 p.m. in a mood alternating between scepticism and hope.

Chapter 3

PETER GETS A LETTER

ALAN arrived back at the farm only just in time for tea; he would, in fact, have been a few minutes late had not his mother, anxious to save him from a second reprimand for unpunctuality, deliberately dallied over the eggs she was scrambling. He was very quiet, though he looked quite cheerful during the meal, and both Mrs. Ferguson and Ella sensed that he was trying to suppress some inward excitement. He was indeed bursting to talk over the result of his visit with someone, and longed to get his mother to himself. The things she found to do seemed endless as she bustled back and forth between dairy, scullery, and kitchen. It was not till much later when Mr. Ferguson had gone down to the village to meet Ella, who had been at a special choir practice, that he was able to unburden himself. First the explanation of his invitation to tea at Woodside Cottage had to be given, though in doing so Alan avoided all mention of Peter Mason. Then came the plan that Mr. Harding had propounded, which was the formation of a club for boys to be run by themselves, and which was to have its headquarters in his house. It would be known simply as "The Pals", and the only obligation of membership should be an undertaking to stand by and loyally help any other member at any time. A table-tennis table could be fixed up in the dining-room, which was at the present time never used; there would be other games available, and a library started. Each member would be free to make use of the headquarters at any time he chose, without reference to special or regular meetings. Outside activities would be organized too. Mr. Harding had pointed out how he himself would benefit by reports and discussions on natural history, in which he hoped a few at least might be interested. He had suggested Alan himself as secretary of this new venture; but of his astonishing proposal that Peter be appointed treasurer, again the boy said nothing. He had indeed been almost staggered himself by the boldness of this idea. Of course Mr. Harding had no real idea of the true circumstances. Peter never had any money and when odd pence had from time to time disappeared from desks and pockets at school, more than one finger had been pointed in his direction. Would it be wise to put him to such a test, Alan had wondered, though he would not for the world have openly expressed any doubts of his friend's honesty. The whole scheme, if only it could be brought about, would be of such immense benefit to Peter; he would be free to sit at Mr. Harding's fire whenever he chose; other boys would by the rule of their membership be obliged to treat him as an equal and a friend. Alan's cheeks glowed with pleasure and enthusiasm as he thought of these things, and his mother smiled and looked pleased too, little guessing the underlying cause of his satisfaction.

"It certainly does seem wonderful that a poor invalid gentleman like that could think of such a thing," she said. "He'll get more than he bargains for, I'm afraid, if he's to have a troop of boys for ever running in and out of his house. His housekeeper'll have something to say to it too, I expect, so don't count too much on it, Alan."

"He's not a bit like an invalid," Alan affirmed, stoutly, "he's got so much go in him. He says he'll be glad of the company and he doesn't mind his things being messed about or anything."

His mother laughed. "He must be a saint then," she declared, "but you go ahead and make the thing work if you can. It's a grand idea."

Mrs. Ferguson was indeed inwardly congratulating herself on the turn events had taken. That Peter Mason would be asked to join the club never entered her head; she believed that Alan's energies and enthusiasms would now find a fresh outlet and that the intimacy between the two boys would die a natural death. So that both she and her son retired to bed that night in a highly satisfied frame of mind.

Sunday was not a favourable day on which to contact Peter. Alan was expected to go to church in the morning and to Sunday School in the afternoon. Ella sang in the choir, so Alan sat by his father in the pew allotted to the Vicar's Warden and family. Mrs. Ferguson never went in the morning, but devoted all her energies to the specially good dinner which always awaited them when they returned. She usually accompanied her husband to evening service, and then it was Alan's turn to keep house by himself. Ella had recently given up Sunday School, declaring that she was "too old," and in any case must have some time to herself on the day of rest, since the choir necessitated her attendance at both services.

As Alan walked down the field after dinner that day, he was assailed by an overwhelming temptation to play truant that afternoon and try to find his friend. It had been arranged that he should bring a few boys to Woodside Cottage for a sort of preliminary committee meeting as soon as possible, and was to call on his way home the following afternoon to let Mr. Harding know when they would be coming. He did so want to talk all these interesting developments over with Peter, whom he had not seen since Friday afternoon. But his mother would be seriously vexed if she ever came to know that he had absented himself in what she would certainly call a most underhand way. His conscience was proving troublesome at the mere thought, and somehow he had a strange though undefined feeling that he wanted the new venture to start with everything straight and above-board. So, with a sigh of resignation, he turned into the church hall and relieved his feelings by being as troublesome as possible during the hour that followed. He quietly drew away the chair from the boy next to him as they sat down after the opening hymn. The resulting confusion was all that could be desired. Edward Moss, a stout, rather lethargic lad, sat down heavily on the floor; the rest of the class and several adjoining ones roared with laughter. Edward groaned and complained bitterly of his injuries; he and Alan kept up whispered recriminations for some time after order had been restored, till their indignant teacher insisted on Alan changing places with the boy sitting next to herself, but even this improved matters but little. The class droned and floundered through "My duty towards my neighbour," as set forth in the Church catechism.

"Please repeat it. 'My duty towards my neighbour is,'" the teacher prompted with some sharpness when it came to Alan's turn.

For a moment he looked blank, then, with a wink at the rest of the boys, he began solemnly, "My duty towards my neighbour is to help him up when he sits on the floor, to—" but he got no further.

The class was once more rocking with laughter, and two bright spots appeared on Miss Daly's cheeks.

"If there is any more trouble with you to-day, Alan Ferguson," she said, angrily, "you can walk straight out. I shall speak to the Superintendent about you afterwards, in any case, but if you're not careful, I'll tell your father as well."

For the time being this threat put an end to any further active trouble. Alan leaned back in his chair, hands in pockets, legs stretched out as far as possible, and gazed up at the ceiling with an expression of profound uninterest. Indeed, since he had been a little chap in the primary class where there had been bright pictures to illustrate stories, and a good deal of cheerful singing, he had never found anything to interest him in Sunday School, and it had not so much as crossed his mind that the teaching he received there could have even remotely any practical bearing on his daily life.

Released at last, he was one of the first to dash out of the building and, turning his face away from home, he ran down the street as far as the tiny cottage where the Masons lived. There was a faint curl of smoke coming from the chimney, but no other sigh of life about the place. Alan hesitated uneasily at the broken gate for some minutes, then at last, with a determined set of his chin, pushed it open, hurried up the path and rapped with his knuckles at the door. It seemed ages to him before he heard the sound of footsteps, and the door opened to reveal Miss Mason's tall, angular figure standing within. She waited expressionlessly for him to speak.

"Is Peter in, please?" Alan asked.

"No, he is not. What do you want with him?" The voice was cold and metallic.

"I just wanted to see him," Alan answered, stoutly, determined not to be intimidated. "Can you tell me where he is?"

Miss Mason uttered a short sound resembling a laugh, but entirely without mirth. "I can just tell you one thing," she said, "he's up to no good. Good afternoon." The door was closed quite gently but with a discouraging sound of finality.

"Horrible woman!' Alan muttered as he turned away. He was again seized with a sense of utter futility. How could anything help Peter when he was obliged to live always with a person like his aunt?

He was surprised to meet the subject of his thoughts just as he turned off the road into the field path. Peter was looking unexpectedly cheerful and was obviously concealing something under his shabby jacket.

"What have you got there?" Alan asked, almost immediately.

With an impish grin the other opened his coat enough to allow a glimpse of draggled brown fur.

"A rabbit! Oh, I say, Peter, I wish you wouldn't! You'll get taken up for poaching sooner or later," Alan exclaimed.

Peter scowled. "Rabbits don't belong to anyone," he defended himself. "I don't believe in those beastly traps, but if I find a bunny caught and dying by inches in one, I guess I've got a right to put it out of misery and take it."

Alan knew this reasoning would not convince his father or any of the other farmers round about, but let the point pass.

"What are you going to do with it, take it home?" he asked, curiously.

"To her? Not much!" Peter answered. "I've got an old saucepan hidden in our shed. I shall make a fire somewhere on the quiet and cook it. Like to come to supper with me to-night?"

"I've got to stay in while the others are at church," Alan said, regretfully, "and I'm late now because I went looking for you. There's a lot I want to tell you, Peter," he went on, eagerly, "but I couldn't find you yesterday or to-day. Come along and meet me on the way to school to-morrow morning."

"What is it?" Peter's curiosity was aroused.

But Alan was firm. "It's a new scheme, but I can't tell you properly here, we'll go into it thoroughly to-morrow," he promised, and so they parted.

Though both boys were early on the road the following day, the talk proved bitterly disappointing. Peter utterly refused to have anything to do with the proposed club or to so much as put his foot inside the gate of Woodside Cottage. Alan's arguments and persuasions were of no avail. He was not going to be patronized "by that paralysed bloke who he had heard was desperately religious," he declared, and, anyhow, the other boys would not join if he did, of that he was quite sure. They both grew hot and angry, and the final bell for school rang while they were still some distance off and on the verge of a really serious quarrel; they had to run then, but tempers were not sweetened by the discovery that the door of the assembly hall had just been shut and that they would be counted late and miss the mid-morning break in consequence. Alan's heart was very sore; it had never crossed his mind that Peter would refuse even to sample the advantages of the new plan. His friend's unreasonable obstinacy and intense bitterness appalled him; some of the things he said had seared like a hot iron. Yet of the two, probably Peter was the most miserable. Alan's friendship was the only softening influence in his life and, as far as he could be said to care for anyone, he loved the boy who alone had singled him out in the midst of a world he had so far found almost uniformly hostile. His pride would not allow him to make the first move or to show any weakening of his hastily-made resolution not to have anything to do with the new club; so when morning school was over, he ran off at once in the direction of his cottage, without giving Alan an opportunity of again opening the vexed question. Not that the latter had any immediate intention of doing so; for once he was glad that no further talk was possible at the moment. He was too sore-hearted to want to mention the scheme to anyone; as for himself, all the zest and enthusiasm he had felt had gone, leaving him feeling deflated and dejected. He wondered drearily what he should say to Mr. Harding that afternoon, for he would have to keep his word and call on the way home from school. He wished he had not been so quick in telling his mother of the plan. How could he explain to her that it had failed almost before its inception?

He hurried to Woodside Cottage at the close of the afternoon, determined to get the unpleasant duty over as quickly as possible. Mr. Harding's reaction to his story of Peter's refusal to co-operate in any way was unexpected. In the first place he refused to share the gloomy and final view of it that Alan had adopted, and secondly he was eager to go on with the plan in spite of it.

"If it's worth doing at all, it's worth struggling for," he said. "You wouldn't want to give everything up because of the first set-back, would you?"

"It was for Peter's sake I was so keen really," he explained, "if he won't come and I do, he'll be more cut off from everyone else than ever."

"I should like to write a letter to Peter," Richard Harding said, suddenly. "What would be the best way of getting it to him, Alan?"

Alan's gloom did not lift. "His aunt would be

sure to get it and perhaps she wouldn't give it to him if you sent it there," he said. "I could take it, of course, but, honestly, sir, it won't do any good."

"If Peter's so obstinate, I don't think it would be the best way for you to be the messenger," Mr. Harding said, thoughtfully. "I know!" he added, "I'll send it through the school. Could you possibly wait while I write? Just amuse yourself any way you like. Then if you would undertake to post it at once, it will get there to-morrow morning, I hope. What is your master's name?"

"You aren't going to write to him, are you?" Alan asked in alarm.

The man smiled reassuringly. "Only a courtesy note to ask him to give the enclosed to Peter. I know Dyer is the Headmaster, but what is the name of the one who teaches you most?"

"Jenkins." Alan looked thoroughly uncomfortable. Peter would be more furious and resentful than ever at having the schoolmaster dragged into what he would term his private affairs. He wandered restlessly about the room, picking up and setting down first one object and then another.

Mr. Harding went calmly on writing, his pen moving rapidly over the paper. Then, having made further enquiries about Mr. Jenkins' initials, he addressed, sealed, and stamped the envelope.

"Look, Alan," he said, holding it out to him, "I'm sure you need not worry that this will do any harm. I'd show you the letter to Peter, only it would be much better for you not to have seen it if he speaks to you about it. I've been praying for him a good deal since Saturday, you see, asking to be directed exactly what to do. I do hope I've not kept you too long and am most grateful to you for helping me to get this off, and don't back out of the club, will you?" he added as Alan turned away.

To this the boy gave no definite reply, but a mumbled "Good-bye," and the assurance that he would run to catch the post. He was still very disturbed by the turn events had taken, but, nevertheless, ran at full speed back to the Post Office, where he let the letter slip from his fingers into the box, with a strong sense of misgiving.

It was unusual for post to be delivered at the school, and Mr. Jenkins eyed the letter that lay on his desk next morning with considerable curiosity as to who his correspondent could possibly be. He had, however, no opportunity of opening it till the mid-morning break. Alan had managed to have a casual word with Peter in the playground as they went into school, sufficient to show that he had no intention on his side of keeping up yesterday's quarrel; and the friends were standing together at playtime when another boy ran up to say Mr. Jenkins wanted Peter.

"What's the row?" Alan asked, anxiously.

Peter shrugged his shoulders. "I don't know, but I suppose he'll have managed to think up something," he said, resignedly, as he moved off. He was back in a few minutes, his face a curious mixture of puzzlement, pride, and defiance. "That bloke has written to me. You put him up up to it, I suppose," he began, accusingly.

"I certainly didn't," Alan declared, stoutly, though not even pretending not to know who was referred to.

"It's queer," Peter said, meditatively. "Want to see it?"

Alan took the letter eagerly, while his pal thrust his hands into his pockets and tried to whistle unconcernedly, horribly afraid of betraying his inward excitement, for this was the first letter he had ever received in his life.

Dear Peter,

I'm sorry to hear our idea of starting a club doesn't appeal to you. Of course that's entirely up to you, but all the same, I hope you will not refuse the favour I'm going to ask. I can't come to see you, so unless you'll come to me, cannot meet you. I'm very keen to do this as you are Alan's special pal, and, having got to know him, I want to know you as well. I'm alone a great deal and if you will pop round to-morrow (Tuesday) evening, or if that's impossible, Wednesday, I shall be waiting for you.

Yours sincerely,

Richard Harding.

The bell sounded before Alan had quite finished and he handed the letter back as they reached the door, with the bare comment, "He's awfully decent, and you ought to see his model planes!"

Peter put the letter in his pocket and went to his place, quite unaware that Mr. Jenkins was regarding him with an interest and curiosity he had never felt before. The covering note he had received had been brief, but had managed to convey a sense of urgency and concern for the boy whom everyone regarded as a hopelessly black sheep. Peter was bright enough in school and could usually more than hold his own with the rest of the class, but his unkempt, often dirty condition, and the bad reports of his general conduct outside, had had the effect of making the master feel that time would be wasted in any attempt to push him on with his studies. Now, for the first time, he gave some serious thought as to what the home surroundings of this unprepossessing pupil might be.

Alan's thoughts too were far away from the lesson. Would Peter accept the invitation, and would any good come of it if he did? Though doubtful on this latter point, he found himself, nevertheless, tremendously anxious that his pal should not show himself boorish enough to ignore such an appeal.

Realizing that over-eagerness might have the opposite effect from the one he desired, he resolutely resisted putting any question in regard to Peter's intentions, when, at the close of morning school, the two walked off together, for though the Mason cottage lay in the opposite direction, Peter decided to go a little way with his friend, and as Alan obstinately remained silent on the one subject occupying both their minds, finally burst out with, "What does he want to see me for, anyway? If he thinks he can give me a pi-jaw, he'd better think again."

"He told you why," Alan pointed out. "He's a chap that means just exactly what he says, I can tell you that. He must be lonely stuck there, never able to walk, and he used to be a fighter pilot."

Peter grunted. "Well, so long. See you this afternoon," he said, and turned back, leaving Alan's curiosity still unsatisfied. Nor did he vouchsafe any more information when afternoon school was over.

Alan was not, however, the only one who would have liked to have asked more questions. Miss Mason regarded her nephew with intense surprise and suspicion. In the first place he was in so punctually that they had tea together, a very unusual occurrence. Afterwards, Peter handed her his jacket, with the gruff request, "Can't you sew up that sleeve and pocket?"

It was an anxious moment, but, assuming that his ragged appearance had been found fault with at school, she grudgingly produced a needle and thread, and, though keeping up a running commentary of complaint and fault-finding, began on the long overdue repairs. Peter made no further move till the jacket was again in his hands, nor did he think it necessary to say thank you. The work had occupied nearly an hour and he was getting anxious about the time. He went out into the tiny back kitchen, shutting the door between, but even so, the unmistakable sounds of shoes being brushed reached his aunt's amazed ears. She did not, however, see the old broken comb being dipped again and again into the cracked bowl of water till the unruly hair at last lay sleek and flat enough to satisfy its owner. She did catch the sounds of the pump handle being vigorously worked up and down, and would have been still more amazed if she could have seen the terrific scrubbing to which Peter was subjecting his face, neck, and hands. Having made what preparations he could, the boy slipped quietly out through the garden, without having to re-enter the kitchen.

He reached Woodside Cottage at about half-past

six, and stood at the gate for some minutes in an agony of indecision. Most people considered him brazen-faced and utterly lacking in reticence, but it took all the resolution he was capable of to enable him to unlatch the gate, and steal softly up to the front door. Whether he would even then have summoned up courage to knock is extremely doubtful; he was, indeed, turning his face uncertainly towards the gate, when the door opened and a woman's voice bade him "Good evening," in a most natural and matter-of-fact manner.

"Come right in, Mr. Harding is expecting you," said Miss Cooper, and, realizing that retreat was now impossible, Peter followed her, blinking slightly as he entered the brightly lighted room.

He would have been amazed beyond words if he had had any idea of the thankfulness and joy that lay behind the quiet words with which the man on the couch near the cheerful fire greeted him. Richard Harding had been praying constantly about this visit ever since he had felt such a strong compulsion to write to this unknown boy; he had taken Miss Cooper into his confidence in regard to his hopes and plans for him, and been promised her full co-operation and support in them. Only two minutes before he had said to her, "Would you mind going to the door, he may be too shy to knock, and if he's not there, leave it open for a little while." And now Peter was really inside. It was an amazing new experience for him, for never in his life before had he been in a really comfortable room; he sat down on the edge of the easy chair by the fire with a mighty effort to appear indifferent and at ease, but was more unhappily conscious than ever before of his shabby clothes and down-at-heel boots. He had planned that his visit should be a short one but it was fully two hours later that he again faced the cold drizzle and darkness of the village street.

He felt in a sort of daze as he moved slowly in the direction of the cottage. The evening had been a revelation to him, and somehow opened up the prospect of an altogether diflerent kind of life. By the time Miss Cooper had brought in the supper tray and set out the low gate-legged table beside the sofa, he had lost all trace of embarrassment, though the thought of eating in such company brought on a return of it, and he was about to refuse, when the fact that this was his host's evening meal, and that he was expected to join it on exactly equal terms, was borne in upon him and checked the gruff denial which had risen to his lips. The good hot soup and the ample plate of sandwiches had been very comforting; nor, beyond the fact that Mr. Harding had bowed his head and uttered a few words of thanks for the food, had there been anything at all of a religious nature to alarm him. For quite a long time the subject of the proposed club was not even mentioned, and then the man had courteously asked his permission to tell him what his ideas had been about it. He laid a good deal of stress on his desire for some members who were really interested in nature, who would bring specimens and information from fields and woods, and be willing to watch birds and animals.

Peter knew that not another boy in the village could compete with him on these grounds, but when the question of the treasurer was referred to, his veto was immediate and uncompromising.

"The chaps wouldn't trust me," he pointed out, the hot colour dyeing his cheeks, "and, what's more important, I wouldn't have any money to put in myself."

Mr. Harding had appeared to weigh these objections carefully.

"We're very much in need of help here," he had said slowly, "though I don't want to press it, or have you think I'm taking advantage of you as a friend, but Miss Cooper really has more than she can manage. If you saw your way to give up a bit of time every Saturday and, if possible, an evening or two in the week as well, to give a helping hand with coal and firewood, and such things, it would be a great relief to us, and we should pay the standard wage per hour As for the boys, those who belong have got to sign the one undertaking, to be loyal pals to each other at all times. You can't be loyal and mistrust at the same time, can you?"

Peter was not quite sure what he had said to all this, nor to how much he had committed himself; he only knew that the warm glow that pervaded his being was not entirely due to his having enjoyed for once a satisfying meal. That he meant to go back was certain. Mr. Harding's manner had been absolutely free of the slightest hint of patronage or superiority; he had, indeed, conveyed the impression that Peter would be the benefactor if he undertook the work he had suggested, and how the boy's heart had leapt at the prospect of being able to earn an honest wage! Not that he had never done so before; in busy seasons he had often spent days in the fields, fruit-picking, and potato-lifting, but his wages had gone direct to his aunt, not one penny into his own pocket. A protest had brought a storm of recriminations down on his head. Was he not obliged to have boots and the second-hand clothing with which at times Miss Mason was compelled to provide him? Did he suppose the few paltry pounds he earned covered the cost of these things, let alone the expense of his daily keep? The boy's mouth took a bitter twist for a moment as he remembered the scenes that had taken place, and he resolved that at any cost his new plans and prospects must be kept secret from his aunt. The back door was locked when he tried it, and before knocking at the front, he deliberately rumpled up his hair and allowed his his shoulders, which he had unconsciously squared as he walked home, to relapse into their usual slouch.

After keeping him waiting for what she considered a sufficient time, Miss Mason opened the door.

"Where have you been out, at this hour?" she demanded, sourly, her eyes darting curiously over him.

It was only quarter to nine, and Peter pushed rudely by her, without vouchsafing any answer, ascended the steep ladder-like stairs, and went to bed.

Chapter 4

THE CLUB AT THE COTTAGE

THINGS began to move quickly after that. Peter went to Woodside Cottage again the next day, his excuse being that he had decided to take the suggested work and wished to know when he could begin. He and Alan went by invitation to tea on the following day, when the club was thoroughly discussed; and on Saturday, four other boys were asked to join them in a preliminary committee meeting.

There was very little active work being carried on among the young people of the village. A few boys who were keen enough had joined the Scouts of the next parish, about three miles off; but for the majority, winter evenings especially were apt to hang heavy on their hands. The new plan was therefore taken up enthusiastically. The idea of a room of their own, a place where they might go, simply by right of membership, whenever they wished, appealed to them strongly, and though after the novelty had worn off it was inevitable that some should fall away, the first few weeks proved rather overwhelming, and Miss Cooper shook her head and declared that her patient was completely wearing himself out.

Mr. Harding had found a staunch helper and loyal ally in Mrs. Stanhope of the Manor House. Though keeping very much in the background where the boys themselves were concerned, she did a great deal to make the dining-room of the cottage into the sort of clubroom its owner visualized. She brought a number of games from her own home which, with her three step-children at boarding school, were seldom, if ever, used. She baked quantities of small plain cakes, and twice a week came to take over tea-making in the kitchen. A cup of tea and a cake could be purchased by the boys at one penny. She had several long discussions with Richard Harding on ways and means of making the club more useful, and particularly on the subject of Peter.

"It is so very strange that somehow I just have not been able to talk to him about the one subject that really matters," he confided to her after the club had been in existence nearly three weeks. "He is interested and bright, and a bit less reserved than he was at first, but unless we can bring him in touch with Christ Himself, what is the good of it all? Nothing else is going to make any permanent change in his life."

"I thought you never found it difficult to turn the conversation naturally into that channel," Mrs. Stanhope said, with a smile.

Richard Harding smiled back. "God opens up the way and He'll do so this time too, I know, if I'm alert enough not to miss my cue when the moment comes," he said. "I've had a good chat with Alan a couple of times, but so far he's determined to avoid a personal issue. Last time he suggested I should talk instead to his sister, who is very troubled about her coming confirmation. It seems her father more or less insists on it and that she feels herself in an entirely false position."

After a little more talk about the Fergusons, they returned to the subject of Peter.

"I tried calling on Miss Mason," Mrs. Stanhope said, "but it was not only horribly difficult but quite unproductive. She is a most forbidding person. She wanted to know why I had come, and simply laughed in my face when I said I would like to know all my neighbours. She said *she* certainly would not, and managed to infer me least of all. She preferred to keep herself to herself, and though she did not actually shut the door in my face, there just seemed nothing to do but come away feeling an utter fool. I'm afraid I'm very stupid at this sort of work," and Mrs. Stanhope sighed.

Richard Harding laughed. "No doubt she's a hard nut to crack. It's little wonder poor Peter is as he is, the surprise to me is that he's not a great deal worse. He has never talked to me about his aunt, his face just darkens if she's mentioned. We shall have to be patient and be content to go slowly, it seems."

Peter was, meantime, facing his own problems. Though he was happier than he ever remembered being before, it was becoming daily more difficult to keep his new prospects and interests entirely secret from his aunt. The fact that he was out of the house a great deal did not in itself rouse her curiosity, as he never stayed in longer than he could help; but several times lately he had come in without appetite for the very unattractive meals that Miss Mason provided. A large cup of cocoa made entirely with milk, with as much bread and cheese as he could eat, in the middle of his Saturday morning's work at Woodside Cottage, made him strangely indifferent to the watery vegetable stew which awaited him for dinner; and his aunt could hardly fail to notice that he swallowed his portion without his usual gusto and did not even look for a possible second helping. Then, on one pretence or another, an evening meal was constantly contrived for him either by invitation to share Mr. Harding's, or in the kitchen if he was working under Miss Cooper's direction. As club treasurer, he had been provided with a cash-box and account book; these naturally remained at the club-room; and in a separate envelope, which he locked safely in the box, Peter deposited his earnings. It was an immense satisfaction to him to turn the key and feel that the little hoard of money was entirely out of Miss Mason's reach. Now a new difficulty confronted him. Mrs. Stanhope had brought a suit down to the cottage belonging to Guy, her younger stepson, which he had outgrown; it was fairly well worn but whole, and greatly superior to anything the boy had possessed before. She offered to sell this to Peter for the sum of £2.50; and there was the money ready to purchase it, honestly earned. Dressed in these clothes, he felt that he could appear more on equal terms with the other boys than he ever had before. Those who came to the club had, for the most part, accepted him as one of them, and abided loyally by the terms of their membership, though not all could entirely conceal their astonishment that he should have been chosen as treasurer. Now came the opportunity to be dressed as well as most of his companions, but with it the certainty of having to let his aunt into the closely guarded secret that he was now a wage-earner. Once this was known he was sure there would be no more peace. He could refuse to give the money up, of course, but he knew to his cost that Miss Mason had various means of retaliation, when seriously annoyed, that could render life almost unbearable; there was, of course, the alternative of making up a story as to how he came by the clothes, but, apart from the difficulty of finding anything convincing enough to satisfy her, he felt a strange new reluctance to gain his ends by lying. Though the club money was very small, his accounts were kept scrupulously, and he sensed a new respect in the other boys as they occasionally looked over his shoulder at the neatness and exactness of the small book, of which inwardly he was intensely proud.

It was Friday evening and Mrs. Stanhope had promised to meet him at Woodside Cottage early, before the other boys were likely to appear, for his final decision about the suit. Peter's mind was made up. Once more he tried on the jacket, that was only the merest trifle too loose.

"It's too cheap, I reckon you're just giving it to me," he commented, rather gruffly.

Mrs. Stanhope hastened to reassure him. "No, certainly not. If you did not buy it, I should either give it away or let some old clothes dealer have it, who would pay even less."

She and Mr. Harding had previously discussed

the question of giving the clothes, and the latter had strongly urged the advisability of encouraging the boy's self-respect by offering them for sale.

Peter looked quite a different person when, with well-combed hair and really neatly dressed, except for the still deplorable boots, he rather self-consciously joined two or three other boys who had arrived in the meantime. He would soon have enough money to buy shoes, but the problem of his aunt remained.

He lingered after the Club closing hour, too ignorant and too absorbed with his own concerns to notice how tired his host was; yet this proved the opportunity for which Richard Harding had been waiting. With somewhat heightened colour, Peter proffered the request that he might leave his new clothes at the cottage so that they might not be seen at home. With tact and patient questioning the man drew out much of the story that the boy had, up to that time, told to no one but Alan. It was getting late and Miss Cooper looked in anxiously, knowing that her patient should have been in bed long ere this. Mr. Harding met her troubled glance with his usual frankness.

"I am so sorry to keep you, Miss Cooper, but I'm afraid what Peter and I have to say to each other to-night won't keep. Please forgive me this once." Then he turned again to his guest. "Your trouble is a big and difficult one, old chap. I can help in very small ways, if you will let me, but I can't do a thing about the root of it all. There is one Person Who can shoulder the whole burden and responsibility, and make a new man of you too, only you've been insulting and ignoring Him up to now, so that He has not had a chance."

Peter stared; then, as an inkling of Mr. Harding's meaning began to dawn on him, grew slowly scarlet.

"I haven't got any use for religion. God's never done nothing for me," he began, defensively, but was silenced by a sharp, "Don't be a fool!" He had never heard the invalid speak in that tone before, and stared in blank astonishment.

It was Richard Harding's turn to speak now and his words were strong and to the point. When, at half-past ten, though by no means willing, he was reminded that he must go, the boy's mind was a whirl of new thoughts and sensations.

"And try to convey my apologies to your aunt for keeping you so late," the man said, as he lay back, his face white and strained with fatigue.

"She'll be in bed. I shan't see her," Peter mumbled, still loath to move.

"In the morning then, and come back to me just as soon as you can," Mr. Harding smiled at him, "but Peter, don't wait for me. Decide your side of this question to-night, alone. Tell the Lord Jesus how much you need Him, ask Him to receive you and make exactly what He wishes of you."

Though Woodside Cottage was open to the club members at any time, it had been made clear to them that Sunday must be regarded as entirely different from the rest of the week, and that none of the games or usual activities would be carried on that day. Any boys who cared to come in for a quiet chat, reading, or writing, were welcome to do so. Neither Alan nor Peter had ever availed themselves of this particular privilege; the former had a fairly full day, and the latter, though longing for something to fill the empty hours, had been too much afraid of being involved in a religious conversation. This Sunday, however, was different. It was a lovely spring day, and Peter, who had spent the greater part of Saturday with Mr. Harding, had again made his appearance shortly after ten o'clock.

Miss Cooper shook her head sadly. "He's just wearing himself right out," she had confided to Mrs. Stanhope the day before. "The doctors were pleased with this place when we first thought of coming, because they thought he'd get all the quiet and rest he needs, but first it was one thing, then another, and since these boys are in and out morning, noon, and night, he's never sure of an hour's peace, and he spends himself out for them, no matter what he suffers afterwards."

Mrs. Stanhope was silent for a moment; she realized Miss Cooper's devotion to her patient, and sympathized with her anxiety. She spoke with some diffidence. "It is such a joy to Mr. Harding to be of use to other people and to realize that though his body is weak and helpless, he can still serve the Master he loves so much," she began. "He knows he is not likely to have a long life and he just wants every minute to be of value."

"Oh, I know," Miss Cooper agreed heartily, "and when he suggested this club and asked me to help, I made no bones about it, but there's reason in everything. He's kept late at night and early in the morning. He won't be able to stand it." The good woman sighed heavily.

Nevertheless, after helping with a few household jobs, Peter spent Sunday morning in, for him, an entirely new way, with Richard Harding.

When Alan came out of Sunday School in the afternoon, he found his chum waiting for him.

"I'll walk up with you," he said, and there was such eagerness and suppressed exuberance in his tone that Alan scrutinized Peter's unusually clean face with mounting curiosity.

"What's up?" he asked as they turned away from the group still lingering at the gate.

Peter did not seem to find it easy to explain and walked some way in silence.

"I don't know how I'm going to make you understand properly," he burst out at last. "I don't understand you anyhow. What made you so jolly decent to me if you're not a Christian?"

Alan positively jumped. "What d'you mean?" he demanded. "Who says I'm not a Christian?"

"I do," Peter affirmed, stoutly. "If you were, you couldn't have kept mum about it all this time. Never mind," he continued hastily as his chum was about to speak, "I *am* now, though I suppose you'll find it difficult to believe, I can hardly believe it myself. It's something so wonderful and extraordinary, I can't put it into words. Mr. Harding told me about it Friday night. He told me what I ought to do then, but

I was in a blue funk. I hardly slept a wink. In the morning it wasn't any better, and I knew I couldn't go on like that."

"Like what?" Alan's tone was incredulous.

Peter grew red to the roots of his hair. His reply came rather low. "Knowing that Jesus Christ was actually calling me to follow Him, and just not answering. I went round to Woodside Cottage again and brought out all my excuses. Mr. Harding showed me what God thought of them and what lies most of them were anyhow. I still felt in an awful funk, but I couldn't hold out any more."

He paused, and Alan asked, impatiently, "Well, so what happened?"

"I asked the Lord Jesus to take me with all my rottenness, and do whatever He liked with me," Peter said, simply, though still very low.

Alan looked uncomfortable. "Ella's gone there this afternoon," he said, suddenly, "I wonder if anything like that'll happen to her. She's all worked up about her confirmation."

"Oh! Perhaps we'd better not go in, then," Peter said, disappointedly; they had almost reached Woodside Cottage.

Alan shrugged his shoulders. "I shan't, anyhow," he said, "I've got to be home for tea." Then, noting his friend's rather forlorn look, he added, "but you needn't mind Ella and there may be some others there, anyhow."

They had reached the gate and stood rather uncertainly outside.

"I say, Peter, do you think this is really going to make any difference to you?" Alan burst out, incredulity still uppermost.

The other nodded gravely. "I wish you could see for yourself," he said. "You may think because you're not a bad lot like me, or even a cripple like Harding, you don't need to be saved, but Christ Himself said you've got to be born again or you can't ever be in His Kingdom, and if you're not in His Kingdom, then you're lost."

"I don't think I'm any better than you," Alan, greatly astonished, affirmed hastily, "but I don't understand that kind of talk. Dad and Mother go to Church and they're good. Dad's Churchwarden, but he never talks like that, and I'm sure he doesn't think like it."

"Ask him and see," Peter said, with a twinkle of merriment in his eyes, as he swung the gate slowly back.

Alan's mouth fell open. "Not much!" he gasped. "He'd think I was absolutely nuts!"

They parted then, and slowly and thoughtfully Alan continued on his way home. He felt quite staggered at what Peter had been telling him and, at the same time, vexed and impatient and, yes, though he did not like to confess it, almost frightened. How could anyone as strong in his views and as determined in character as his pal have veered round so completely in his outlook, as it seemed, overnight? Of course Peter had been bad and his lack of so much that others took for granted in life must make a difference; in spite of his quick denial a few minutes before, Alan began to feel that perhaps, after all, religion might do something for one so destitute and needy, and for whom nothing but disgrace was predicted by most of the villagers.

He had soothed his disturbed feelings into his more usual condition of cheerful complacency by the time he reached home, and did hearty justice to the home-made cakes which always graced the Sunday tea-table.

Mr. and Mrs. Ferguson set off for Church a little early, as Mrs. Ferguson wanted to enquire for a sick neighbour on the way, and Alan, having poked the fire into a cheerful blaze, in spite of the mild evening, settled down to read his library book. Faintly in the distance he could hear the peal of the Church bells; they sounded pleasantly soothing and unreal. How glad he was that his parents did not require him to attend the evening service. Though fond of company, he was usually perfectly contented by himself for these Sunday evenings. There were a few small jobs to be attended to, according to season, and the supper, which was always cold, to lay ready for the churchgoers' return. It was only a little after half-past six when he was startled to hear the back door open softly and familiar quick, light steps, as Ella walked into the kitchen.

"What's the matter with you? Why aren't you at Church?" he greeted her accusingly.

She stood smiling at him in a way he found odd and, somehow, disconcerting; looking at him for a moment without saying anything, she passed on through the room, put away her hat and coat, returned and sat down on the low fender stool.

"I've got something to tell you," she began.

Alan groaned. "Oh, my hat!" he exclaimed, "another of them!"

His sister stared at him in astonishment. "What do you mean?" she demanded. "You don't know what I'm going to say."

"Oh, yes, I do. At least I don't know how you're going to say it, but I bet I know what it is. Go on, cough it up." With an air of resignation he leaned back, folded his hands, and closed his eyes.

Ella was considerably taken aback. "If you're going on like that, there's not much use trying to tell you anything," she said severely, "but I did want to, because I've told you how rotten I felt about the confirmation, and, and for other reasons too," she ended rather hurriedly. There was a long pause.

Alan opened his eyes. "I don't hear anything," he declared solemnly.

"You won't either." Ella jerked out the words, sprang up and fetched a book which was lying open on the old sofa, then she resettled herself by the fire and began to read, keeping her face well screened from her brother, lest he should catch the glint of tears, half of anger, half of disappointment, which had risen to her eyes.

"Oh, go on, don't be a mutt," the boy protested. "I'll listen with all my ears, honestly I will." It took some little coaxing on his part, however, before his sister was sufficiently placated to lay down her book.

"This isn't a joke, Alan," she said seriously. "You know I told you some time ago that we weren't Christians, and just going to Church and behaving properly doesn't make you one. I know, because there were one or two girls at school who were real. They've left now and I never paid much attention to them when they were there, but they did teach me that much. The more I've thought about it these last weeks, the more miserable I've been. The Vicar's classes haven't helped at all. He asked us the catechism questions and all that, but it didn't mean a thing to me. I just couldn't explain to Father, and yet to go through with it seemed impossible. Besides," Ella flushed and hesitated a little, choosing her words carefully, "I wasn't satisfied. I wanted something real, but I just didn't know the way to find it and was afraid as well."

"What of?" Alan asked curiously.

"Of what it might mean," his sister spoke gravely. "I'm still a bit afraid, I think," she confessed, "even though it's all settled now."

Alan kicked the fender. "What's settled? I wish you'd speak out and say things in plain words. I don't know what you're driving at."

"Don't you? You said you knew what I was going to tell you." Ella's clear grey eyes searched his face. "Well, listen. The Lord Jesus is our rightful Owner and King, first because He is the Creator, He made us, but then He came to save us from the awful sin and mess that we'd got into, and make us doubly His own. Yet even now He won't force us, but just calls us to follow Him, and to every one who answers and asks Him to receive them, He gives eternal life, and much much more even now in this life." Alan was staring open-mouthed and the girl hurried on. "That is what I've done, asked Him to take all my particular sins away and receive me, and I have promised that in future I'll only obey and follow Him. That's why I'm still a bit frightened of all that it's going to mean." Somewhat deflated with the effort this speech cost her, Ella was quiet for a few moments, then, as her brother did not seem inclined to speak, asked in rather a small voice, "What did you mean when you said, 'another of them'?"

"I guess Peter Mason's caught the same fever as you," he said calmly.

"Peter Mason!" Ella's tone expressed the utmost amazement. "That awful boy!"

"If you're going on being snooty about him, I shan't tell you anything," Alan threatened. "Look at the time!" he added, springing to his feet. "They'll be home in a few minutes."

However, while they laid the table he consented to report something of what Peter had told him that afternoon, and found his sister's intense interest and astonishment somewhat soothing to his strangely ruffled feelings. Alan could not possibly have explained why he felt vexed and irritated at the turn events had taken; indeed, he would not have admitted that such was the case. He told himself that it was no business of his, and that he did not care in the least, but underneath there was an odd sense of loneliness and being left out, as if the other two had somehow got beyond him. He had by no means answered all Ella's questions in regard to Peter's experience when they were interrupted by the arrival of their parents.

Chapter 5

DIFFICULT MONDAY

WITHOUT attempting to analyse his reasons, Alan took considerable pains to find excuses for not going to the Club for the next few days, and even at school did not see as much of Peter as usual. Peter was exceptionally quiet and appeared preoccupied. Some of "The Pals" twitted him with what they termed his moodiness; they missed his lively wit and smart repartee, which had, in spite of his many disadvantages, given him an assured place and even a certain amount of leadership among them. Peter, however, was fighting his own battle, seeking to adjust himself to the completely new set of ideas and values that had come into his life. Except for the weekly Scripture lesson at school, he knew absolutely nothing of the Bible; now, having been given one of his own, he began to read it for himself. He was alternately shocked, amazed, and appalled by what he found in it. Mr. Harding privately declared that his comments and questions were an education in themselves; but it was well for Peter that he had a friend and teacher who never sought to evade an issue, or to advance his own superior wisdom.

"See here," the boy began somewhat aggressively on the following Sunday afternoon, "if this means what it says, I reckon there ain't any Christians left in the world now." He pointed an accusing finger at the thirty-third verse of Luke 14, and Richard Harding read the words slowly.

"So likewise, whosoever he be of you that forsaketh not all that he hath, he cannot be my disciple." He looked up to find that his questioner's mood had changed, his eyes danced with mischief.

"I haven't got anything except Aunt Agatha. I'd like fine to forsake her!" Peter affirmed with mock solemnity.

The man laughed heartily, then he read the words again. "The Lord Jesus always means just what He says, you know," he said meditatively. "Tell me what you make of it."

The boy shook his head. "Well, if it means just that, there aren't any Christians. That's what I don't understand, 'cos *you* are, anyhow, and there's Mrs. Stanhope, and Tom Hargreaves says he is now."

"And you, too," Mr. Harding chimed in. "You know the Lord Jesus has accepted and saved you, don't you, Peter?"

"Yes, I thought I did," the boy hesitated a little, "but this is so queer."

"You need not have the slightest doubt about that," the man went on quickly, "because He said that He would not cast out anyone really coming to Him, but, having taken you, He wants to make you His disciple indeed, and a disciple is one who learns of and follows his Master. Well then, as you read more of your Master, you'll find that He would let absolutely nothing get in

His way of going to the cross. Satan tried to stop it, and so did His own family and His dearest friends and disciples, as well as all the natural shrinking in Himself, but He just kept steadfastly on. I'll show you some of the passages in a minute. Then he told His disciples that they must take the same position, and not expect to be above Him. He called it taking up the cross every day, and I think that is what He means here. People are prevented from following Him truly, honestly and fully, by so many things, and if they won't let go any thing or person at all, no matter what, if they get even a little bit in the way of this following, then, though He has saved them, He can't call them His disciples and friends."

Peter's eyes never left the speaker's face; there was a deep furrow of concentration between his brows as he listened.

After a little silence, Mr. Harding added, half to himself, "The things that do get in the way are, very strangely, often the ones we would least expect, and it is more strange still that we are so unwilling to renounce them."

"What have I got to renounce?" the boy asked, his tone a mixture of defiance and awe.

"Your pride," the answer came unhesitatingly, "your bitter feelings, in fact your entire attitude towards your aunt."

"It's impossible! You don't know her." Peter spoke hotly.

"Quite impossible for you," came the quiet agreement, "but with God all things are possible, and you have God with you now, so you can do this and very much more."

The talk went on. One or two boys arrived, looked in and quickly went out again, for boys often have more tact and consideration than they are given credit for. Miss Cooper brought a tea-tray to the door, and silently carried it back to the kitchen. It was more than an hour past the usual time when Peter came out to her.

"Mr. Harding says he's very sorry to have kept you so late, and if you'd like to go to Church now, I can do everything." His tone was unusually subdued.

"You only need to make some fresh tea. I'll just go and see him," the housekeeper said as she hurried in to her patient. "You've had that boy here since before two o'clock, now it's half-past five!" she began reproachfully.

"It's well worth it," he replied tranquilly, "I think the Lord has wonderful plans for that boy."

To Peter, however, the way that lay immediately before him looked anything but wonderful. It had never even occurred to him to tell his aunt of the change that had come into his life, nor could he think of any more impossible task. Not that he was really much concerned with what her reception of such a surprising revelation might be, he was on the whole genuinely indifferent to either her jibes or her ridicule; but the very fact of beginning a confidence in a house where any form of normal conversation had long been unknown, seemed to him a feat absolutely beyond his power. His pride, though never till to-night had he recognized it as such, recoiled in horror at making the first move in any such direction.

"I can do all things through Christ which strengtheneth me," he said to himself rather grimly as he walked back towards the cottage. "I shall see whether that's really true or not in a few minutes. If I can do this, I guess I can do anything."

He had left Woodside Cottage as soon as Miss Cooper returned from evening Church, and it was not much after eight o'clock when he pushed open the one-hinged gate. The small oil-lamp was lighted, and stood on the bare table. It had been a mild day, but the evening was decidedly chilly now; nevertheless, the grate was empty. Miss Mason sat in her usual place, upright in the wooden armchair; she had a shawl round her shoulders, and looked cold and pinched. Every time the boy came back from his new friends, the contrast both in outward and inward things struck him like a blow in the face. To-night it seemed worse than ever, and his newly awakened spirit, now made more sensitive, quivered and shrank as he looked first at the silent figure by the cheerless grate, and then round the depressing room. He sat down on the opposite side of the hearth, but though this was in itself an unusual proceeding, Miss Mason made no sign that she had noticed his presence. The silence grew more oppressive every moment, and feeling the last remnants of his courage slipping from him, Peter burst into speech.

"Aunt Agatha, I'm sorry things are so rotten. I want them to be different." It was not in the least what he had meant to say as, on his way home, he had tried to plan the interview, and even to himself his voice sounded strained and unnatural.

Miss Mason did just vouchsafe him a glance, then as she replied in her chilliest and most sarcastic tones, "Oh, indeed! You would like a good many things, I've no doubt. What do you propose to do about it?"

Peter flushed. No matter how tightly he held himself in, his aunt always had the power to make him angry; he simply must not show resentment now.

"Mostly by being different myself, I hope," he answered quietly, and somehow he felt that the words came without any conscious direction on his part, but he could add no more. His throat felt constricted and his eyes smarted.

After waiting a few moments in unbroken silence, he rose and made his way up the steep narrow stairs. He threw himself face downwards on the bed, striving to fight back the unmanly tears that threatened to overwhelm him. The temptation to such weakness was a new experience. He had early learnt to control all outward show of feeling, save that of anger or contempt, since there had been no one to care whether he cried or not; but the sense of frustration and of anti-climax, as well as bitter disappointment with his own first attempt at personal testimony, was proving too much, and for a little while silent though convulsive sobs shook him from head to foot. Had he but known it, he had left his aunt hardly less shaken than himself. She too had for many years so schooled herself to suppress all show of feeling, that even had she wished it now, the habit held her in chains she was powerless to break. She was completely bewildered by her nephew's declaration of his hope of "being different," though she tried to dismiss it with a shrug of her shoulders, saying sourly to herself, "The only difference I'm likely to see in him is for the worse."

So the two partook of their usual silent breakfast next morning, and if Miss Mason noticed that sticks had been chopped for the fire, and water drawn, she did not betray the fact. Not that Peter generally refused to perform these tasks, but he seldom did them without a reminder, and to-day there was a good supply of wood, and the fire already set for lighting. Nor did he follow his usual custom of rushing out of the house the moment the last crumb was swallowed, but hung about as though he would like to say something, if he could but find the words. The school bell began to ring at last, and he was obliged to go. Dissatisfied and depressed as he felt on the surface, he was, nevertheless, conscious that the change he had experienced more than a week ago was fundamental, and that the new troubles and anxieties which beset his path could not altogether disturb an inward peace, which had deepened since his long talk with Mr. Harding on the previous day.

The trials of that Monday had, however, hardly begun. After the mid-morning break, the whole school was summoned to the Assembly Hall instead of returning as usual to their classrooms. The Headmaster and all the staff were present. Merely stating that he was extremely sorry that such a proceeding was necessary, Mr. Dyer ordered every boy to fold his arms behind his back. Then, each in turn was to empty the entire contents of his pockets, placing the articles they contained on the floor in front of him, under the supervision of his Form-master, and then resume the position of standing with arms folded behind. Only a few had any idea of what article was being looked for and the long search went on in silence, save for the rustle and clink of the motley assortment of oddments found in the various pockets being laid on the floor, and the occasional shifting of feet or embarrassed cough among the waiting boys. It was over at last. Mr. Jenkins, standing at the end of the line of boys who comprised his form and keeping an eagle eye on them that nothing be touched, addressed the Headmaster.

"Mason has a pound."

Every eye in the room was instantly turned upon Peter, who lifted his head and stared back defiantly. He did not understand what the trouble was about, but his heart had begun to beat quickly.

"Is he the only one?" Mr. Dyer asked.

It seemed that he was. There was a fair number of pennies and five pence pieces, and three fifty pence pieces among the curious mass of articles that had formed the contents of the boys' pockets, but not another pound. There was an uncomfortable pause, then the order was given for the boys to pick up their belongings and go to their classrooms.

"Mason, come to my room," the Headmaster added sternly.

"Thief!" one boy managed to hiss as he passed, and Peter clenched his fists as he turned to obey the summons to the room that held nothing but painful memories for him. He had appeared there several times during his school career, usually for mischievous practical jokes, or deliberate insolence, and twice for playing truant.

Mr. Dyer sat down and looked the boy over coldly. He noted that his appearance was tidier than on former occasions; he was not, however, disposed to deal leniently with one who had been a constant source of trouble, and his voice was somewhat harsh as he began.

"My advice to you, Mason, is to speak the truth at once. It will save you, as well as others, a great deal of trouble in the long run. I can't, of course, promise not to punish you for such a serious offence as theft from another boy, but the punishment will not be so severe as it will if you add lying to stealing."

Peter's face had turned very white; he gazed back at the Headmaster in hostile silence.

After a considerable pause Mr. Dyer rapped his desk impatiently. "Come now, when did you take this money from Alfred Long's pocket?"

"I didn't take it." The words were little more than an angry whisper, and the obvious resentment expressed in the none too respectful tone did nothing to ease the tenseness of the atmosphere.

"Don't talk nonsense," the master rasped. "Long came to me with the report of his loss only ten minutes before I called the assembly, and you are the only boy in the school with a pound in his possession. Surely you've sense enough to see for yourself that lying can't help you in a case like this."

"I'm not lying. That's not Long's pound, it's mine!" Peter asserted doggedly.

Mr. Dyer realized that he was in danger of completely losing his temper, and took a firm grip on himself.

"Look here, Mason," he said evenly. "You're behaving like a young fool. You surely don't want me to call in the police and have you dealt with in Court. Why don't you own up and take your punishment like a man? I never thought you were a coward."

The quieter tone was not without its effect. The angry boy had a sharp moment of realization that once more the pride of which Mr. Harding had had so much to say the previous evening was proving his worst enemy, but none but God Himself could know what a bitter battle with self was fought in the next few moments.

Naturally, the master took his silence for continued obstinacy and, after waiting a reasonable time, asked coldly, "Well, are you going to tell the truth or not? This is your last chance."

Peter swallowed hard and moistened his dry lips; for the moment, certainly, he had every appearance of guilt, but now his voice was firm.

"Yes, sir, this is the truth. I earned that pound with the work I do at Woodside Cottage. I don't know a thing about the one Long has lost."

Mr. Dyer was plainly startled. He looked hard at Peter. "Why did you not say that at first?" he asked.

"I was riled at being called a thief," the boy answered bluntly, and again the man stared hard at him.

"You realize, I suppose, that your statement about earning it can be checked up on," he said gravely.

Peter merely nodded.

"Even if that proves true, is there anyone who knows that you had this in your pocket when you came to school this morning? For if this is yours, we have still not accounted for the one Long says was taken from his jacket pocket, in the few minutes he was without it while practising high jump in the playground."

"He put it down on the ground, I saw him," Peter agreed.

The master, secretly somewhat surprised at this admission, leaned back thoughtfully. "Tell me exactly what you saw and what happened," he demanded.

"I saw Long take off his jacket and throw it down with some others." Peter spoke with quiet assurance. "I watched the jumping for a minute or two, then I went away."

Mr. Dyer rose. "I want you to show me exactly where this happened," he said, and together they went out to the playground.

The boy pointed out the scene of the jumping and, as far as he could remember it, the exact spot where the pile of discarded jackets had been placed. The master and he then began to go over the ground almost inch by inch, but it was Peter's quick eyes that spied the missing coin which had evidently fallen out of Alfred Long's pocket when he threw down the jacket, and rolled some distance; it had been stopped by the high playground wall, at the foot of which small tufts of grass and weeds were pushing between the bricks and trying to grow, serving as an effective hiding-place.

"There it is!" Peter could not quite keep a note of triumph from his voice, nor did he pick up the money till he had pointed out its exact position.

There was an awkward silence. Mr. Dyer, who was feeling decidedly mortified, cleared his throat.

"I'm sorry, Mason," he said rather formally, "this was a most unfortunate occurrence. Long did not tell me that he had put his jacket on the ground, only that he took it off for a very few minutes. Now please return to your classroom and tell him to come to me."

It was not an easy order to obey, to go to his place and carry on as if nothing had happened, while the rest of the boys still believed him a thief.

"He ought to come with me and tell them," Peter muttered to himself as he approached the door.

Of course every eye in the room was turned upon him the moment he entered, but without a glance at any of them, he walked up to the desk and delivered the message that the Headmaster had sent to Mr. Jenkins. As he turned away from the desk, he tried to catch Alan's eye, but the latter had his head bent diligently over his book and did not look up. A little cold fear clutched at Peter's heart; if his own special pal believed him guilty, he felt that there would be little point or satisfaction in being vindicated before the rest of the school A surge of bitterness swept over him. He thought he had finished with all this sort of thing and that henceforth his life would appear honest and unblameable before the world, but instead things were worse than ever. He told himself that if Alan, with whom the solemn vow of friendship and loyalty to each other, no matter what happened, had been taken, should fail at the first real test, he would never trust a human soul again; but even as the dark thoughts crowded in, he remembered that he now had a Friend Who would not fail and Who, he had been assured, could be trusted at all times. Would Christ really stand by him now? he wondered. As he and the Headmaster had walked out into the playground, he had prayed quite desperately for success in finding the shilling. Was the fact that he had done so indeed an answer? The bell for the close of morning school interrupted his thoughts and there was the usual rush for the door. Several boys ostentatiously turned their backs on him; a few talked loudly about the rottenness of having thieves at school; not one spoke to him.

He had already turned homeward when Alan's familiar quick step overtook him. He was looking awkward and distressed.

"I say, Peter," he began, "I'm awfully sorry about this. Do tell me what really happened."

Peter scanned his friend's face narrowly. "Will you believe me if I do?" he demanded. "Tell me yes or no, do you think I took that money?"

Alan flushed. "I'd stick by you whatever you'd done, you ought to know that," he declared. "There didn't look as if there could be any two ways about it, but I don't believe you'll tell lies to me."

Peter's brow cleared a little. "But you think I would to other people," he commented with something like one of his old impish grins. "Well, I can't blame you for that, I suppose, only I've done with lying for ever. You're a real pal, Alan. I was the rotter to doubt it." Hastily, for time was short, he outlined what had happened.

Alan had to run then, but even as he sped along, his thoughts were busy. There was a change in Peter; in his sister too, perhaps an even more marked one. Ella was so anxious that he should share her experience that, to use the boy's own phrase, she nagged him on the subject whenever they were alone, but Alan was strangely reluctant to be drawn into discussion, though as a general rule he dearly loved an argument; deep down, there was a sense of irritation towards both his sister and his pal, which at times almost amounted to hostility. They had gone on to something he did not understand (nor wish to), and he was left standing outside, with a sense of frustration to which he was unused, and would most certainly not admit.

Meanwhile, the troubles of that Monday, which Peter had envisaged so very differently, were not yet over. Miss Mason and he ate their usual silent dinner; to-day it consisted only of bread and dripping and tea. Afterwards Peter went up to his room, a most unusual procedure;

but the power of prayer at all times, in every circumstance, had been so impressed upon him by Mr. Harding, that, feeling the need of strength and calmness to face whatever developments afternoon school might bring, he determined to try the experiment. The moment he entered the room he saw that the Bible, which for the first time he had left on the broken chair by his bed, was missing; up to that morning he had carefully hidden it under his mattress each day but, disappointed in his effort at confession to his aunt the previous evening, he had determined at least to allow the openly displayed Bible to speak for itself. Now it was gone! Peter stood quite still. There was no possible hiding-place in the bare little room which, beside the bed and chair, contained absolutely nothing but an old box in which the boy stored an odd assortment of treasures. Feverishly he turned over the contents, stripped and searched the bed, his anger mounting momentarily. He was turning to rush downstairs when something checked him. The row he was proposing to have with his aunt would certainly not impress her with the reality of the change that had taken place in him, but how could he hold back the flow of hot words that seemed literally pressing on his lips in an effort to pour out? He passed his hand across his brow. He had come up here to pray. What a mockery! Turning back, he knelt down beside the bed, but he was trembling with wrath and no articulate words would come. Soon the school bell began to ring. Peter stood up then and went softly to the top of the stairs; there was no sound below and he crept down. A quick glance showed that the room was empty, and with a sigh of relief he hurried out. He caught a glimpse of Miss Mason bending over the vegetable plot as he ran down the path.

There was no general assembly for afternoon school as a rule, but to-day, after the register had been taken in each class, the boys were directed to go into the hall. A wave of excitement swept over them. What new development had taken place? One whispered the information that Peter Mason was to be publicly thrashed, another that the police had been called in. There was a moment of tense silence when all were in their places. Then Mr. Dyer cleared his throat.

"Long and Mason, please step out here," he said. Both boys looked uncomfortable and self-conscious as they obeyed the summons. "It was necessary to have the whole school together," the Headmaster went on, "as a grave injustice was done to one of you this morning, before all of you. Peter Mason was not guilty of stealing, or of lying, and Alfred Long wishes to apologize publicly to him for the trouble he has caused."

Looking as if nothing could be further from his wishes, Alfred murmured a few almost unintelligible words, and Peter, much taken aback and very red in the face, assured him that it was quite all right.

The boys found themselves back in their classrooms less than five minutes after they had left them; they were, however, restless and inattentive. Those who had been most ready to cry "Thief" in the morning were subjected to a good many black looks. Alfred Long was besieged by whispered questions from his nearest neighbours. Some of the more thoughtful boys realized that the trouble was not so completely over and done with as the Headmaster supposed. The story had been related at many dinner-tables that day, and was certainly all over the village by this time. This, indeed, proved to be the case.

Miss Mason, going down to the general shop to make a few purchases in the afternoon, was confronted with it.

"Sorry your nephew's in trouble again," Mrs. Robinson said, as she weighed up the small portion of cheese. Her customer looked up but made no reply. "A terrible thing when a young boy takes to stealing," the good woman continued unabashed, "small sums now and people may overlook it, but it's bound to lead to serious trouble if it's not checked in time."

"What are you talking about?" Miss Mason demanded angrily.

Mrs. Robinson handed the parcel across the counter with a shake of the head. "I'm sorry if I've said the wrong thing, but I thought you'd be sure to know by this time. Peter stole a pound from another boy's pocket this morning, was caught red-handed with it, I hear."

If she hoped to produce a sensation, she was disappointed. Miss Mason merely took the parcel and stalked, without a word, out of the shop.

"She's as bad as he is. No manners at all," the little woman muttered to herself, then turned eagerly to discuss this latest tit-bit of gossip with the next customer.

Peter had determined to thrash out the question of the missing Bible with his aunt on his return from school but he was also resolved to keep his temper at any cost while doing so. He was very hungry, for bread and dripping coupled with strong emotions do not prove a lasting or satisfying standby. The moment he opened the door, however, he knew that things were going to be more than usually difficult. The table was completely bare and the atmosphere charged with hostility. Nevertheless, he advanced boldly and stood squarely before his aunt.

"Aunt Agatha, what have you done with my Bible?" he asked evenly.

The words seemed to release a long-pent-up torrent. "How dare you!" Miss Mason fairly screamed. "You were bad enough before, heaven knows, but I'll have none of your religious pretence here. I've put the Bible in the fire, where it belongs. 'Where's my Bible?' you miserable little hypocrite, with all the village pointing its finger at you for the thief you are!"

"Oh!" Peter caught his breath sharply. "You've heard that too, have you, and you didn't stop to find out any more? It's not true. As for thieves, the book you burned wasn't yours, was it?"

"You—" with all her force the furious woman struck her nephew in the face. The blow was so unexpected that Peter reeled backward and almost fell; his teeth had cut deeply into his lips and the blood came freely. It was a long time since Miss Mason had resorted to any actual violence, and she braced herself now for the wild onslaught she fully expected; but Peter turned without a word or look and went out at the door.

His aunt sank down in her chair; she was trembling. It had been a trying day for her too. She hardly understood herself the impulse that had made her burn the Bible she had found on the chair at Peter's bedside that morning. Secretly, though she would never have admitted it, she had felt extremely uncomfortable about her hasty action all the morning. When the boy had gone upstairs, she had taken a sudden decision to work in the garden, rather than meet him face to face when his loss was discovered. But the brief visit to Mrs. Robinson's shop had altered everything. What a fool she had been to regret her action! During the hour she had waited for school to be out, her anger had continued to mount till it reached white heat; that Peter had actually taken the initiative and accused her acted like a match to gunpowder. Now she felt quite weak and spent. She even wondered dully where the boy with his bleeding mouth had gone, and if people would see and question him about it. Then she set her lips, and composed her face into its usual expression of cold immobility.

Chapter 6

MISS MASON REMEMBERS

PETER turned his back on the direction of Woodside Cottage. Much as he longed to do so, he was not going there in his present disordered condition, indulging in self-pity and looking for sympathy. He felt more forlorn and dejected than he ever remembered. The fact was that the day had been a very trying and exhausting one; he was tired, hungry, and thoroughly discouraged. He held the piece of rag he used for a handkerchief to his mouth and walked slowly on. There were only two or three detached cottages standing some distance from each other, before the end of the village street merged into the country high road. His eyes were on the ground, and he did not even notice a woman standing at the gate of the neat cottage he was passing, and started sharply when his name was called.

She was a short, rosy, pleasant-faced woman, and she opened the gate and spoke eagerly. "I'm glad to see you, Peter. I just wanted the chance of telling you how sorry I am for what happened to-day. Alfred's told me all. He acted too hastily. But what's the matter with your face, my dear?" Her voice took on a note of concern.

"It's all right," Peter answered rather grimly. He realized now that it was Mrs. Long who had addressed him, and would have gone on, but she laid her hand firmly on his arm.

"Come in and have a wash, you can't go about like that," she insisted, and wonderingly Peter allowed himself to be escorted up the path and into the house.

This kitchen was not much larger than the room he had just left, but what a contrast it presented! The stove was brightly polished, and the kettle sang on an old-fashioned hob by the fire. The clean, coloured tablecloth set off the willow-pattern cups and saucers. Geraniums bloomed in the window. A large tabby cat sat washing his face on the gay rag hearthrug.

Alfred, who, hands in pockets, was evidently waiting for his tea, looked somewhat taken aback at the appearance of the unexpected visitor, but his mother did not give either boy time for embarrassment.

"Bring the kettle, love," she addressed her son as she hurried Peter through to the tiny scullery, "we want some warm water to bathe these nasty cuts." Very gently she went to work, exclaiming in horror as, pulling back the lower lip, she saw the extent of the damage. "I'm afraid you've been fighting, Peter," she said reproachfully, when she had done all she could. "Is the other boy hurt as much as you are?"

Peter managed a rather wry smile. "I haven't been fighting this time, Mrs. Long, and thank you very much."

She scrutinized his face hard as he turned to go, then made up her mind. "I don't know how much you can manage to eat with that bad mouth, but you must stay and have tea with us. I'll boil you an egg nice and soft and it will go down easily."

Utterly dumbfounded, the boy could only stand and stare at her. Never in his life before had he received such an invitation. Woodside Cottage he set apart in his mind as something altogether different, but that the mother of one of his school-fellows should ask him to sit down with them at their table startled and amazed him.

"Shan't I be a bother?" his face was red, and his voice rather gruff.

"Of course not, we're right glad to have you." Mrs. Long turned hastily to her preparations. She had heard much evil of this boy, and up till to-day would certainly not have run the risk of doing anything that might make for friendship between him and her own son, but she had a tender heart and a strong sense of justice, and when Alfred had given her a full account of the day's events at school, her imagination entered with surprising accuracy into something of what Peter's feelings must have been. Then when she had seen him coming down the road, his forlorn look of weary dejection had moved her strongly, and his plight called out all her natural pity and tenderness. If he had not been fighting, and somehow she was strongly inclined to believe him on this point, who could have given him such a violent blow?

Alfred tried somewhat awkwardly to make the guest feel at ease, and Peter responded as well as he could, though greatly handicapped between shyness and his severely torn lip. When the meal was over, he would have liked to show his appreciation by at least helping to wash up, and followed Mrs. Long out to the scullery, but Alfred's two sisters got on with this as a matter of course.

"I'd better be going. Thanks a lot," he began, and paused uncertainly.

"Come and see us whenever you feel like it," his hostess said warmly. She sensed there was something else the boy wanted to say, but did not know quite how to draw it out.

"She must be a Christian. I wish I could have asked her," Peter said to himself as he turned back along the village street. Other club members would be making their way to Woodside Cottage now, and he felt he could go there with an easy mind. He spent most of the evening in the club-room, only looking in to say good-night to Mr. Harding when leaving.

"Come to tea with me to-morrow, Peter," the man invited warmly. "I've been hearing something about your troubles at school to-day, and am jolly glad it was cleared up so quickly, but I'd like to know what you have to say yourself, and you've not been in all evening."

"Yes, I'll come," Peter promised thankfully. He kept his face in the shadow, and if Richard Harding noticed his swollen mouth, he made no comment.

Peter walked homeward very very slowly. Mrs. Long's kindness, and the cheerful atmosphere of the club, where the boys had been specially friendly and cordial to him as if anxious to make amends for the earlier injustice he had suffered, had done much to soothe and comfort his sore heart; but his feelings towards his aunt were still intensely bitter, much more so on account of the destroyed Bible than his own physical hurt. There were moments when he felt that the odds against him were too great, and the Christian life an impossible one; yet the thought of turning back to the old existence was impossible too, and he knew that some change had been wrought in him which was fundamental. He turned aside presently, taking a narrow lane and then over a gate into a quiet meadow. Throwing himself down in the shelter of the thick hedge, he gazed up for some time at the dark sky, till the serenity, majesty, and glory of the stars seemed to creep into and enfold his whole being. Then he turned on his face and tried to pray. Peter could never have passed on to another, however sympathetic, either the reality or wonder of that solitary experience. For the first time in his life he was consciously in the actual presence of God. Awe, reverence, and joy filled him in equal proportions, and when at last he rose up to go, there was a quiet confidence in his face that had never been there before. He could face his aunt now, for the bitterness had somehow been washed clean out of his heart; not that he would be likely to have to face her that night, it was past ten o'clock, and having little or no occupation for leisure hours, Miss Mason usually retired to bed extremely early. He wondered if in her anger she had barred the doors against him, and, if this was the case, whether he would be able to get in. Not that it seemed to matter very much, he would find somewhere to sleep. It had been an extraordinary and harrowing day, and he was very, very tired.

The back door, however, was on the latch and there was actually bread and margarine on the table. He felt no desire to eat, but was astonished that the provision had been made for him. As a matter of fact, Miss Mason had for once been somewhat uneasy in her mind. She knew that the bread and dripping dinner had been inadequate and had secured an egg for her own tea, which she had made sure of getting well out of the way before her nephew's return. Her anger at what she had heard, had, as usual, taken the form of refusing him a meal; but the blow had been unpremeditated, and Peter's reception of it had somehow left her shaken and secretly ashamed. She had made herself a cup of tea before going to bed, and had thus furnished herself with an excuse to leave something on the table. Peter looked curiously at the things, then put them carefully away and crept noiselessly up to bed.

There was silence as usual between them the next morning, though Peter racked his brains for something to say. Such was their strange relationship that there seemed to be absolutely nothing on which he could even make a casual remark in a natural manner. He turned, however, when he was leaving for school.

"Mr. Harding has asked me to tea this afternoon, so I shan't be in." The words were bald enough, but his voice was quiet and pleasant.

"Getting grand friends, aren't you?" His aunt's

tone was acid. "Perhaps Mr. Harding won't be so pleased to have a thief in his house as you seem to think."

The blood rushed into the boy's face, he stood still, looking at his aunt with flashing eyes. He went to the door, then deliberately turned back and spoke quietly. "I don't know who told you that story, but whoever it was didn't tell you all. I didn't take that pound, and it was proved before the whole school yesterday." Then he left her.

In spite of herself, Miss Mason found that she actually believed her nephew was speaking the truth. Almost she decided to go down to the shop and tell Mrs. Robinson exactly what she thought of her gossiping tongue, but her knowledge of the actual facts was too scanty for her to be certain of coming best out of such an encounter, and she decided against it. She was altogether puzzled over Peter. She was amazed that he had not struck back at her the day before; nor had there been any of the foul language she would have expected under such an attack. It was obvious that he was making a real effort to be pleasant to her and, though she had no intention of responding, she was uncomfortable and disturbed.

At dinner-time he twice attempted to start some sort of conversation, to which she replied in monosyllables.

After school Peter walked with Alan as far as Woodside Cottage. "Are you coming down to-night?" he asked.

"I don't think so, I might," Alan replied evasively.

Peter eyed his chum narrowly. "You aren't as keen about it as you were at first," he challenged. "What's up?"

"Nothing." Alan kicked a stone. "We aren't bound to go every night, are we?"

"No, but you don't come much now and you've got some reason. You might as well tell me," Peter persisted.

"There's nothing to tell," Alan's tone was slightly grumpy, "but if you really want to know, there's too much religion there for my liking."

Peter stared in astonishment. "That's rubbish!" he affirmed. "No one talks religion to you if you don't want it, and, anyway, why are you so afraid of it? I do honestly want to know why you aren't a Christian, Alan."

The other boy gave an exasperated little laugh. "There you are, you and Ella between you are enough to drive a chap bats! Who says I'm not a Christian? You both seem to know more about me than I do myself."

They were standing at the gate of Woodside Cottage by this time, and Peter would have burst into further eager speech, but Alan checked him.

"Cheerio, I've got to run!" With a friendly thump on his friend's back, and a wave of the hand, he made off at full speed, leaving Peter looking after him with puzzled eyes.

In reality he was not more puzzled than Alan himself. As he slowly climbed the last steep field to his home, his mind went back regretfully to the happy carefree existence he had been leading up to a few weeks ago. His thoughts never troubled him then. Now it seemed as if everyone was pushing the same question at him in one form or another; by everyone he meant Mr. Harding, Peter, and most of all his sister. He did not want to answer that question or even admit that it needed an answer, but however determinedly he thrust it away, it would keep cropping up with an irritating persistence. Even his mother had quite unwittingly raised it again when she asked what had come over him to make him so snappy and disagreeable to Ella. Alan sighed and resolved for the hundredth time not to allow himself to be disturbed by anyone else's strange views; he stuck his hands deep into his pockets and began to whistle.

Peter went home early that night. He walked into the cottage with an air of quiet determination, and confronted his astonished aunt.

"Look, Aunt Agatha," he began without giving himself time to hesitate, "I've got another Bible, because I must have one. I won't leave it out if you don't like to see it, but please don't touch it."

Miss Mason's mouth opened slightly and for a moment she struggled for speech. "Where did you get it?" she demanded at last.

"Mr. Harding gave it to me," Peter answered quietly. "You see, he helps me to understand it, and he says a Christian simply can't do without reading it every day."

Conflicting emotions almost choked his listener. "A Christian! You don't call yourself a Christian, do you?" Without waiting for an answer she hurried on. "So you've been whining and telling tales to that cripple, trying to get him to pity you. I knew this club and going to work there, and all the rest of it, would lead to something like this. I've always kept myself to myself and had no gossip and no interference, and now like the mean sneaking little cur you are, you go off talking behind my back and telling whatever lies you fancy for your own ends. A Christian indeed! Well, I'll have no Christians here, nor Bibles either!"

Peter regarded his aunt thoughtfully. He did not in the least understand her and, up to the present time, had certainly never tried to do so; but now, as he looked at the hard lined face, with the bitter drooping mouth and weary discontented eyes, instead of the anger and resentment which her outbursts had hitherto never failed to call forth from him, he felt something very like pity stir in his heart.

"You've got it all wrong," he said quite gently. "I told you the other night I wanted things different, it's because I'm different. As the difference works, you might even like me a bit better."

He was answered only by a contemptuous snort, and Miss Mason flounced round in her chair, turning her back to him.

Just for a moment the boy stood gazing at her wistfully, then he went slowly upstairs and, sitting down on the bed, tried to think things over dispassionately. He did not really believe that his aunt would refuse to have him any longer in the house, but she certainly could, if she chose, make life almost impossible for him. If she did mean it, how very different everything would be. His heart gave quite a leap at the thought. If she really turned him out, he could leave her with a clear conscience; he knew there would be shelter and friendship, and the love he had never known since his father died, at Woodside Cottage. Only after the long talk he had had with Mr. Harding that evening, he had returned with an entirely new sense of duty and responsibility, determined to shoulder the burden cheerfully, and try to make something of his life with his aunt.

As for Miss Mason, she sat quite still in the old Windsor chair, staring straight in front of her, while her thoughts explored the past with relentless accuracy. She thought of her brother as a little boy. She was a good ten years older than he, and she had loved him with a fierce and jealous love, which had deepened and become more possessive when their mother died. The boy had then been seven years old and Agatha had deliberately set herself to make him as dependent upon her as she possibly could. As he grew older she continued to come between him and any intimate friendship, especially girl friends, for a number of years. Until he was twenty-five, she had succeeded in keeping him almost entirely to herself, and had grown skilful in the art of breaking off any incipient friendships he seemed likely to form. The cottage was a neat, cheerful place, with a well-kept garden in those days. Robert Mason was cowman at one of the largest and most prosperous farms in the district. In his spare time he helped her to cultivate their little plot, and took pride in the fine vegetables and flowers it produced. Then Marjorie Langford had come to stay with her aunt at the village

Post Office, and from the moment he laid eyes on her, it seemed to Miss Mason that her years of devotion and care for her brother, together with the influence she had acquired over him, all counted for nothing. Marjorie was eighteen. Her sparkling, dark eyes always seemed full of laughter; her soft, red lips curled into smiles almost without provocation; her small, graceful figure moved about the village with a joyous energy, and she had an interest in everything which was all her own. Agatha Mason fought hard, but it was a losing battle; indeed, she herself hastened its inevitable end by the bitter hostility, that rapidly grew into actual hatred, which she openly displayed for the girl who had captured her brother's heart, and whom he obviously adored. Mrs. Brown, of the Post Office, was not sorry to have the responsibility of her extremely pretty orphaned niece off her hands, and the marriage was hurried on. Miss Mason refused to attend the ceremony or to allow her brother to bring his bride back to the cottage; though she could not legally have prevented this, Robert was unwilling to subject his wife to the unhappiness such an arrangement would have certainly caused, and yielded to her eager request to seek work in the city where she had been brought up. Four years later he returned, broken in heart and health, a widower with his three-year-old son. Miss Mason received them, secretly glad that sorrow and pain had forced Robert to return to her, but from the first moment the child, who laughed up in her face with the merry dark eyes which were so exactly like his mother's, whose quick, light movement and carefree exuberance reminded her at every turn of the girl she had hated, was a new object of jealousy and dislike. Her brother openly adored the little one and, fearing to lose him again, the sister was this time wise enough to hide her animosity in some measure at least. It was, however, soon obvious that Robert's days were numbered, and as his strength waned, his eyes rested on his little son with an ever-increasing tenderness and anxiety. The cottage was still partly his, and this, with a small sum in the Post Office, he had made over to Peter. Again and again during the last weeks of his life he had sought a promise from his sister that she would care for the boy.

"There's no danger of my turning him out in the street, is there?" she had answered sharply on one occasion, and the weary, pleading look in the hollow eyes of the sick man came back to her now with a mingling of remorse and resentment. She had never tried to comfort the child's wild grief over his father's death, or given him a tender word or look. She had cared for his physical needs fairly conscientiously at first, but as his proud little spirit developed, refusing to be quelled by the crushing methods she applied, she saw more and more of his mother in the boy, her dislike had hardened and crystallized, and the habit of brooding resentment grew upon her. Resolutely she shut herself and the child off from their neighbours; the garden was neglected; the house grew more shabby and uncared for; the bitter barrier of misery and hatred behind which she had entrenched herself now seemed impenetrable. She moved restlessly at last and tried to shake off the dreary haunting memories and to relapse into the apathetic indifference in which she was accustomed to enfold herself. Though Peter strongly resembled his mother, there had been something of Robert in the way he had spoken to her that evening, something too of the hurt, defenceless look she had sometimes seen on her brother's face during the last months of his life. Miss Mason rose at last and turned with a determined effort towards the stairs.

"He won't reform," she told herself resolutely. "It's just a bit of novelty because he's taken up with that Mr. Harding and his precious club. What has a boy got to do with religion, anyhow? I never did and never shall believe in it."

Nevertheless, had Peter known it, his Bible was safe from that time forward.

Chapter 7

"NOTHING SHALL BE IMPOSSIBLE"

A YEAR passed swiftly. It had brought little apparent change to the external life of the village; but in Peter Mason none would have denied that there was a vast difference. To begin with, his outward appearance was now what the neighbours termed thoroughly respectable; while his industry and readiness in accepting any kind of honest work that offered was often held up as a pattern to other boys. He certainly earned his living, in spite of the fact that he would not be allowed to leave school for another year. He had opened a Post Office account, though no one but Richard Harding knew of its existence, and the book was in his safe keeping. No one else guessed anything of the determination and self-sacrifice that went in to each shilling resolutely scraped together and deposited in this account, nor of the purpose which lay behind it; long, earnest, and absorbing conversations took place between the two on this subject when no one else was present.

Miss Mason was as dour and silent as ever, she showed no interest in her nephew's comings and goings, and never questioned him as to his plans or wishes. The meals she served were, however, a little more regular, and for some time the calm of the household had been undisturbed by any open conflict between them. Not that Peter had as yet gained perfect control over his temper, nor his aunt lost either the desire, or the power, to rouse and hurt him. There were times when the boy flared almost as fiercely as of old into bitter speech and furious retaliation, but each time this happened his aunt's taunts at the pretence of his Christian profession, her sneers at his inconsistency and the hypocrisy of people in general who considered themselves better than others, called him to a sudden halt, ashamed that he had given any encouragement to one of her favourite themes. Unwittingly she had thus helped him to attain a greater measure of self-control than would have seemed possible in any ordinary circumstances to one of his temperament under constant provocation, for, young as he was, Peter had reached the place where the honour of his Lord was very dear to him, and to have smirched it in any way a real grief.

His friendship with Alan Ferguson remained on an uneasy and unsatisfactory basis. Both boys were too obstinate and tenacious to give it up, but Alan still remained outside the things that now made Peter's life, and neither could look to the other for the full entering into and sharing of interests and ideas that they longed for.

The Club flourished, though, as seems inevitable with all such projects, subject to many ups and downs, setbacks and encouragements. Out of it had grown a nucleus of four or five really Christian lads, who met with their leader for regular happy times of prayer and Bible study, and who were on the look-out for opportunities of reaching others, whether members of the Club or not. These were energetically backed up by Mrs. Stanhope's two stepsons when they were at home from school and college; while their sister, Beryl, now nearly fifteen years of age, found many quiet ways of helping. But those who knew and cared for him most were beginning to realize that the central figure, around which all this young life and activity seemed to revolve, was not likely to be with them much longer.

It was a lovely evening early in the summer holidays, and Peter was busy picking raspberries in the garden of Woodside Cottage. Mr. Harding was suffering from one of his bad turns, and had not been able to receive visitors for the past two days. Glancing up, Peter was surprised to see Beryl Stanhope standing outside the back door. Rather startled, he picked up his basket and came out from among the canes.

"Hello, Peter!" Her smile of greeting was warm and friendly; they had got to know each other remarkably well during the last summer and Christmas holidays.

"I've just been in to see Uncle Dick."

She had always called him that, but something in her tone now made him look at her questioningly, and as she remained silent, he asked, or rather stated with almost impatience in his voice, "He's better, then?"

"Miss Cooper says he's better than yesterday," the girl was choosing her words carefully, "but he's very, very weak and so tired. Peter, he does want to go so much, we can't try to keep him." There was a little tremble in her voice, and she turned her head away and looked out over the garden with a quick blink of the eyes.

There was silence between them for a full minute. Peter's face was white, and when he spoke his voice was gruff.

"It's all right for you to talk like that, you've got everything, father, mother, home. If Mr. Harding goes, there isn't anyone left for me," and he turned hurriedly away.

"Oh, Peter, no!" the girl was quick to protest. "There's no one like Uncle Dick, I quite agree, but God won't ever leave us quite alone, the Lord Jesus promised it."

The boy did not respond; he plunged into the midst of the raspberry canes and continued picking fiercely. Beryl stood hesitating; she longed to be able to bring some comfort to the sore heart of the lad who, it seemed likely, would so soon be called upon to part with his only real earthly friend; but what could she say? Words appeared empty, and she turned sorrowfully away, her own heart heavy with the thought of the impending separation.

"Mother will help Peter all she can, I know," she said to herself, "but I don't think he really loves anyone but Uncle Dick." She shivered slightly as she looked round the familiar kitchen. What would it be like to have Woodside Cottage empty of its tenant?

Miss Cooper came from the sick-room and smiled at her. "Well, your visit seems to have done him good, my dear," she said cheerily. "He is certainly better this evening."

The girl's face lighted up. "Oh, I'm so glad,

but, Miss Cooper, he seemed so weak, even since the last time I saw him he has changed."

The housekeeper nodded. "He loses more with each setback than he gains," she admitted sadly.

"Do try to say something to comfort Peter," Beryl pleaded, "I don't think he knew just how ill Uncle Dick is, and I upset him dreadfully."

"Poor boy, it'll go hard with him," Miss Cooper sighed, "he just worships Mr. Harding and no wonder either, but all the village will be the poorer for his going."

Peter did not come in for some time. When he did, he set the basket down in the scullery, and asked Miss Cooper in a very subdued voice if there was anything else she wanted done that night. She replied in the negative, but added hastily, as the boy would have immediately left, "As it's Saturday to-morrow, try and come in early and help me pick them over. If Mr. Harding keeps up the improvement he shows to-night, you'll be able to see him for just a few minutes."

The boy's face lightened a little. "Do you think he's really better?" he asked, with a suppressed tenseness in his tones, which spoke all too eloquently of his inward emotion.

Miss Cooper regarded him with pitying eyes. "Yes, I do," she answered stoutly, after a moment's hesitation. "If the improvement keeps up, you'll be able to see him for a few minutes to-morrow."

With a decidedly lightened heart, Peter turned into the deserted club-room, got out his books, and tried to apply his mind to study. For the past year he had, under Mr. Harding's tuition, been working steadily to improve his education and was already well in advance of the top standard work at the village school.

"Miss Cooper knows a lot more about illness than Beryl does," he comforted himself. "It's just like a girl to look on the black side of things."

The promised visit to the sick-room was paid next day, and though Peter was shocked and secretly alarmed at the effect the few days' severe illness had produced on the invalid, he found Richard Harding as cheerful as ever, and eagerly interested to hear of all his doings since they had last met. He talked of going over some of the exercises and an essay Peter had written that evening, but the boy drew back. "They must wait. Don't bother about me, sir, I can still get on with something."

Mr. Harding smiled. "I'd like to do it if I can, all the same," he persisted. "You're getting on grandly and it would be a pity for anything to keep you back. I want to do my part while I can."

Peter had to go with those last words sounding in his ears, "while I can." Was his friend, too, trying to warn him that he would not have his help much longer? Fiercely and determinedly Peter thrust the thought from him. He was not ready yet to face up to the question of what life would be for him without the refuge of Woodside Cottage, and the friendship of its master. Nor was that by any means all, it seemed to him that all his efforts after a better education, all the secret plans and ambitions which he and Mr. Harding discussed and worked for, and of which he had spoken to no one else, must come to an end. How firmly he had believed that those plans were of God, yet at the thought of the human instrument being removed, his faith in their accomplishment utterly failed.

As the summer days slipped by and the invalid was once more found on his couch in the garden he loved so much, the boy's fears were lulled to rest. He was very busy. The farmers had plenty of work for willing hands, and at the end of the first week of school holidays, he came in late Saturday evening with glowing face.

"I've got five pounds to put away," he announced proudly.

"That's great. I know you must have been at it pretty hard, I haven't seen you for days," the man responded heartily, "but what does your aunt say about it?"

"She wanted to know about the money, of course, she always does, and I gave her two pounds. She has hardly had to give me anything at all to eat this week, but I told her I was saving every penny I could get."

"Didn't she ask you what for?" Richard Harding asked curiously.

"No, just said it was a pity I was a miser as well as everything else, but she wasn't bad really." Peter spoke with a matter-of-fact cheerfulness, and for the hundredth time the invalid regarded him with a mixture of wonder and pity. That the lad, scarcely more than a child, could maintain his buoyant outlook in spite of the dreary and unnatural conditions of his home surroundings, was a continual source of amazed thankfulness to him. He had often considered asking Miss Mason to pay him a visit, but the dread of doing the boy harm instead of good had held him back from carrying out the plan, far more than her nephew's assurances that the invitation would most certainly be refused.

"I'll put the money in my book and take it to the Post Office first thing on Monday," Peter went on. "That'll make £25.75p," he added, after scrutinizing the book carefully, though he knew every entry by heart. "It'll take a long time to get enough for my training. I hope I won't be too old by that time."

Mr. Harding laughed, then he said quite gravely, "You sound as if you had to depend on your own efforts. If God wants to take you out to preach the Gospel, He won't be short of means to do it."

"No, but I've got to earn the money for it, haven't I?" Peter spoke positively.

"We don't know that," his friend replied. "I'm sure you're right to try your best and do your part, but not to think that is the most important thing, or that it all depends on how much you can earn. Faith that can't believe when there seems no possible way is not faith at all."

Peter turned this over silently in his mind for a moment or two. "But I don't see how I can ever go to College without paying for it," he burst out.

Mr. Harding regarded him with a twinkle in his eye.

"The Israelites didn't see how they could ever escape with Pharaoh's hosts behind them, and the sea in front," he said. "As long as you keep in exact line with God's will and plan for you, nothing shall be impossible for you. The Lord Himself said it. Don't insult Him by doubting His Word. Your first and all-important job is to be so in touch with Him that you can be sure of the way He is leading you." He leaned back with a little sigh, watching Peter's still somewhat puzzled face. "Come in for a real good confab to-morrow, it's late now, but there are several things I want to talk over with you."

Peter said good-night and turned away, with one last anxious glance at the weariness which could not be hidden on his friend's white face, and at the deep lines of pain about the firmly set mouth.

The long afternoon that he spent at Woodside Cottage on that quiet summer Sunday marked another milestone in Peter's life. Richard Harding talked to him of the Lord, Whom he himself was soon going to see, in such an utterly natural and happy way that the boy's dread of the impending separation slipped for the time being into the background. Heaven, the Father's house, the reality of Homegoing, the joy and triumph, the pleasures for evermore, made his face glow with anticipation; he found himself envying the man who had so nearly reached the journey's end.

"We're only passing through, it helps so much to remember that when things are difficult and painful," Mr. Harding said, "but it's even more important to remember it when they're going well, there is such danger then of settling down as if we really belonged here, and were not just strangers in a foreign country on our way home. It seems as if God has to be constantly doing things to remind us. He could not make me realize or even believe it till He had taken away everything I thought made life worth living; since then He's given me a hundredfold more, and now this supreme thing far above all, that I shall see Him face to face. I don't think He'll need to deal with you like that, but don't ever let your own plans and ideas get in the way, specially your pride, Peter. It will mean dying daily to get absolutely rid of that."

"I thought I was rid of it. I hardly ever—" the boy began, then checked himself and laughed rather ruefully.

Mr. Harding chuckled too. "It crops up again in a wonderful way and in so many different forms, I know," he said. "For instance, when I'm gone, it might easily take the form of shutting yourself up and not letting other people help you, when they are more than ready to do so."

"I don't want other people," Peter muttered rebelliously.

"There you are, God may want to use others in carrying out His plan for you, but your pride could spoil the whole thing, only you won't let it, will you, old chap?"

The boy's head was down. There was a long pause before the answer came. "No, I won't. I'll fight it every day, no matter what way it comes."

They talked on for some time, then when it was obvious that further talk was impossible for that day, Richard Harding said, "There is one thing I want you to do right away, Peter, I mean to-morrow or as soon as you can, that is, get Alan to come and see me once more."

"I'll try. I don't see how he can *not* want to, but he's very queer sometimes." There was a mixture of doubt and impatience in Peter's voice.

"Pray for him just as much and as strongly as ever you can," the invalid urged, but his voice was scarcely more than a whisper, and Peter stole quietly away.

He had a job on a farm not very far from the Fergusons the next day, and presented himself at the back door at a very early hour. Ella was setting the breakfast-table in the kitchen, and she greeted him with a friendly smile; but Mrs. Ferguson, who came out of the dairy at that moment, found she had not quite got over her prejudice against Peter, and to the request, "Can I see Alan, please?" merely pointed to the yard and answered somewhat brusquely, "He's somewhere about with his father, I think."

Alan came into sight carrying a pail at that moment and Peter hurried up to him.

"Mr. Harding wants specially to see you," he began, with only the briefest of preliminary "Hullos." "Will you be sure to go down and see him to-day?"

"We're awfully busy. I don't think I *can* go to-day. What's it about?" Alan was obviously reluctant.

"Alan," said Peter sternly, his voice hoarse with the emotion he was determined not to betray, "don't you know that Mr. Harding is awfully ill? The doctor doesn't think he'll live many more days. You'll feel pretty rotten afterwards if you put off going too long."

His friend flushed uncomfortably. "Oh, all

right, I'll go, but if he's so ill, I don't see why he wants me to come bothering. I don't know what to say to ill people, anyhow. I expect he'll get better too," he added as an afterthought, "everyone's thought he was going to die lots of times before."

"When will you go?" was all Peter said to this, his mouth firmly set.

"This evening. I can't get away before. I don't see what good it'll do, anyhow." Alan muttered the last words as, with a hurried "Cheerio," Peter ran off.

"What did that boy want?" Mrs. Ferguson enquired as Alan washed his hands at the sink, preparatory to sitting down to breakfast.

"He says Mr. Harding wants to see me and that he's going to die in a few days," her son replied bluntly.

With an exclamation of distress, Ella flew out from the kitchen.

"Is he as bad as that? Did he *really* say that, Alan?" she demanded.

Her brother merely nodded.

"I knew he'd had a bad turn and that they were very anxious," Mrs. Ferguson said with a sigh, "but he's pulled round wonderfully before and may again. I daresay Peter was making the worst of it. Come along now, your father's ready."

Ella Ferguson was an early visitor at Woodside Cottage. She returned to the farm with such shining eyes and such an unusually exalted look about her face that her mother glanced at her curiously several times before she enquired, "Is Mr. Harding better after all?"

"I don't think so. He couldn't talk very much, but, oh, Mother, he's so glad to be going to Heaven, I think he's half there already."

Her mother actually looked a little shocked.

"We all know he's ready to go, of course," she admitted after a pause, "he'll be greatly missed, but I suppose it's a happy release for him if he is taken."

Ella turned and looked fully at her mother. "Don't you think it's happy for everyone who knows they're going to the place the Lord Jesus has actually prepared for them Himself?" she asked.

Mrs. Ferguson was greatly taken aback. She stooped and looked critically into the oven.

"Healthy people don't want to die," she answered, her face flushed from the heat of the oven, "and it's not natural for young people to think about such things. I don't want Alan getting all upset and worked up about it."

"But, Mother, there can't be anything unnatural or upsetting if we know we are just going Home to the Person we love best, and as everyone has to die some time, don't you think it's tremendously important to know that it will be *just* going Home?"

"Yes, I suppose so," Mrs. Ferguson sighed uncomfortably, "but Alan's a good boy really, there's no harm in him, and I can't see much gained by stirring up all his feelings."

Ella checked the rush of words that came to her lips; she felt so entirely helpless to make her mother understand. She turned away to lay the table, but there was a little tremble in her voice as she said, so softly that Mrs. Ferguson hardly caught the words, "Alan doesn't know the Lord Jesus as his Saviour, and that is all that matters."

When Alan presented himself at Woodside Cottage that evening, Miss Cooper met him at the door with a very anxious face.

"Mr. Harding insists on seeing you, my dear," she explained, "but you must only stay a very little while. He's really past seeing anyone, but he keeps the same right to the end, he won't think of himself."

Alan drew back in alarm.

"I won't go and disturb him, I'll call again to-morrow," he said hurriedly.

Miss Cooper shook her head.

"No, he's expecting you, and there may not be a to-morrow."

She opened the bedroom door and almost pushed the reluctant boy inside, closing it gently behind him. Though quite unused to sickness, Alan was instantly aware of the change that had taken place in the man on the bed. He was lying flat, instead of being propped up as usual; his face was so thin it looked almost transparent, and his eyes were deeply sunk; only his smile of welcome was the same as ever, as he held out his hand to his very scared-looking visitor.

"So glad to see you, Alan." The voice was very feeble but distinct. "I can't say a lot. I'm just waiting, you know, for the Lord to give the word of command and I shall go to Him. It's so marvellous, no words can express the joy and wonder of it." He paused for breath, but the radiance that shone in the tired eyes proved the reality of the joy of which he spoke.

Alan stood in awestruck silence; he could think of no possible word to say. The conventional "I'm sorry you're so ill" which he had planned was obviously out of the question. After a few moments, Mr. Harding continued. "I've been thinking about you a lot, and wondering why you are still holding your life back from Jesus Christ. Are you willing to settle that question now?"

The pause was much longer this time. At last Alan murmured unhappily, "I don't know."

A shadow fell across the sick man's face.

"That means no," he said sadly, "but I'm not going to press you, because you must not take this step to please me or anyone else, only, Alan, will you solemnly promise me that you will face up to the whole matter this week? Don't wait any longer, or dare to make light of what the Lord Jesus has done for you, and remember nothing less than your all will do for Him. Get Ella to help you if you need any help." The man's voice was scarcely audible and Miss Cooper, who had returned, was hovering anxiously in the background.

"Come now," she said softly, stepping forward; but Richard Harding somehow managed to hold out his hand again and as Alan took it, whispered, "Will you make me this promise?"

"Yes, sir, I promise," the boy said gravely.

The man smiled, and Alan felt a slight pressure of the hand he held. "Thank you. Good-bye, Alan."

Out in the quiet village street, where the shadows looked dark, thrown by the rays of the setting sun, the boy felt strangely stilled, almost awed. He turned his steps very slowly in the direction of home. He had made no binding promise, he assured himself firmly as he tried to regain his usual cheerful indifference to the great question that had again been pressed upon him; he would keep his word, of course, but not with any interference from Ella, he knew only too well how eagerly she would seek to influence him; yet his feeling of disturbance and unsettlement persisted.

It was the baker who brought the news to the farm the next day. Mrs. Ferguson turned away from her chat with him with a somewhat perturbed face, and when Alan ran in a few minutes later for a mid-morning snack, she watched him eat in silence till the last crumb had disappeared, then she said quietly, "Mr. Harding died last night, Alan, only two or three hours after you left him. You must have been the very last person from outside to see him alive."

Utterly dumbfounded, the boy stared back at her, his face paling under its deep tan.

"I didn't think he was *really* going to die," he said at last, and getting up walked slowly into the sunshine that somehow seemed to him to have lost its warmth and brightness. It was the first time that Alan had been in close contact with death, and the fact that the man who had been talking to him so naturally and cheerfully only a few hours before was now actually dead, shocked and profoundly disturbed him. The promise he had made assumed a much deeper significance in his eyes; he felt he would have to carry it out with scrupulous care. A promise to the dead must be honoured at all cost.

Chapter 8

"I'LL LOOK AFTER YOU"

IT was the day of Richard Harding's funeral. Miss Mason had just watched the departure of her nephew, looking very spruce and neat in well-brushed suit and carefully polished boots. He had told her that the service would be in the church at eleven o'clock, while he was getting ready. The actual news of the invalid's death had reached her through Mrs. Robinson. Peter had been very silent during the intervening days; there was a stricken look in his eyes that brought tears to those of Mrs. Stanhope when she saw him, and which even his aunt could not fail to notice, though as usual she made no comment. Now she felt strangely restless; though she would not own it to herself, she wanted to see the funeral procession, and, after some inward conflict, decided she might as well go down to collect her bread from the shop then as any other time. The cortège would pass directly by its door on the way to the church. She left plenty of time so that her call at the shop might appear entirely casual, and so as to avoid waiting about. Finally, she took her basket and set off briskly. Arriving at her destination, she was pulled up sharply. The shop was shut and the street seemed strangely deserted; glancing up towards the church, only about a hundred yards away, she was amazed to see that the churchyard was thronged with people. It seemed that practically the entire village had turned out to do honour to the man who, since his arrival some six years before, had never once been able to set foot among them. Now the hearse came into sight. Miss Mason drew back hastily. She had no desire to stand as a solitary spectator at the side of the road. The curtains in the cottage next to the shop were closely drawn and no one appeared to be about; the porch afforded just the shelter she needed and she slipped thankfully into it.

It was a very simple procession. Mr. Harding had no near relatives and, by some, had been considered a very solitary and lonely man. His doctor and solicitor, with Miss Cooper, Mr. and Mrs. Stanhope, and one or two others, drove behind the hearse. Then came a procession of boys—Miss Mason thought nearly all the lads of the village must be there—and leading them, walking very erect and with eyes staring straight ahead, her own nephew Peter, with Alan Ferguson at his side. A very odd sensation indeed stirred in Miss Mason's bitter, self-centred heart; she hardly knew what to make of it. Could she possibly feel pride in the nephew she had so persistently disliked and scorned, the son of the woman she had hated? She was assailed by a most disconcerting desire to follow the crowd into the church. She had not been to church since she was a young girl, and was certainly not going to yield to any such crazy fancy, she told herself indignantly. Nevertheless, when the coast seemed clear, she went up to the churchyard, and, skirting round its outside, took up her position behind the hedge only a few yards from the newly dug grave. A considerable group of people were already standing beside it, for the most part waiting in reverent silence for the last act of the burial service. Presently they came, and again Miss Mason was amazed at the crowd which followed the coffin. A little cluster of girls took up their position at right angles to where the unseen watcher stood, and immediately after the solemn words of committal, their voices, clear and sweet, rang out on the summer air.

On that bright and golden morning when the Son of Man shall come,
And the radiance of His glory we shall see;
When from every clime and nation He will call His people home;
What a gathering of the ransomed that will be.

When the blest who sleep in Jesus at His bidding shall arise
From the silence of the grave and from the sea,
And with bodies all celestial they shall meet Him in the skies;
What a gathering and rejoicing there will be.

Miss Mason had no idea of how hard Ella Ferguson had pleaded with the Vicar to allow this innovation. She did not even know that this burst of triumphant song was an unusual feature at a funeral, but as she looked at the girl's glowing face, uplifted to the sky as she sang with all her heart in her voice, heedless of the drops that still hung on her eyelashes, the strange upsurge of unaccustomed emotion, which seemed so persistently to assail her that morning, came to a head. She turned resolutely away, forced to blink her eyes to rid them of the moisture that even to herself she would not own called for the use of a handkerchief, and, forgetting her errand, went straight home with all possible haste. She wondered when Peter would return and, albeit with a scornful twist of the lips at what she termed her own foolishness, she fetched an old piece of clean tablecloth and predared the midday meal with unusual care.

It was some time before her nephew arrived and when he did his face looked so bright that a sarcastic remark about the evident pleasurable effect of a funeral rose to his aunt's lips, but was not uttered, for Peter's eyes had gone straight to the neatly set table, and he turned at once to her with a smile of warm appreciation.

"It looks nice," he said simply.

Miss Mason flushed. "We might as well live decently, seeing you've smartened yourself up so much," she muttered, as surprised at her own words as Peter was to hear them. "You don't look much as if you want cheering up, all the same," she added with thinly disguised curiosity.

Peter was silent as she put his plate before him. He bowed his head for a moment, a habit to which his aunt had become accustomed during the last few months, though at first she had deeply resented it. When he opened his eyes, he met hers frankly.

"I wish you could understand how glad I am," he said.

"Of course *I* can't be expected to understand you or your grand friends," she retorted sharply. "I was mistaken to think you were worrying yourself over Mr. Harding's death."

Peter did not flinch under the bitter words. "I'm sorry," he answered quietly. "I'm glad because Alan Ferguson has given himself to the Lord Jesus, and I wished you knew what a wonderful thing that is." There was utter silence after that till Peter spoke again as they rose from the table.

"Mr. Harding's solicitor asked me to call at his office to-morrow, so I shall have to go by the nine o'clock bus. I can't think what he wants to see *me* for."

Miss Mason stared at him in astonishment. "He must have left you something," she exclaimed, "unless," she added suspiciously, "you've been up to some mischief."

The "he" of course referred to Mr. Harding and Peter made no attempt at an answer this time; he experienced another of those choking uprushes of desolation in the realization of all that his loss meant. Quickly he picked up the plates and carried them into the scullery; in silence he dried the dishes for his aunt, and for once it was she who longed to ask questions, and who had to hold in a desire to give some verbal expression to her amazement.

Afterwards he went out to the tiny shed in the garden, where he was at the moment carefully nursing a rabbit with a broken leg. Among some of the boys, the Club had done much to stimulate interest and care for all living things and they had got into the habit of bringing any they found lost or injured to Peter, whose almost uncanny skill and dexterity in handling them was giving him quite a name in the village. These creatures had been housed in an outhouse at Woodside Cottage, until Mr. Harding's death, where their special patrons could always have access to them and watch their progress, but now Peter, very thankful that at the present he had only one patient, had removed the rabbit to the shed.

When Peter departed the next morning to catch the bus, his aunt actually unbent sufficiently to give him some advice, the first he could ever remember receiving from her.

"You be careful," she said, "don't let yourself in for anything. You can't trust lawyers."

An hour or so later Mr. Jennings, the solicitor, leaned back in his chair, and rather quizzically surveyed the bewildered boy who faced him across the mahogany desk.

"Is there anything you don't understand?" he asked kindly enough, though for the last twenty minutes he had been carefully explaining the clauses in his late client's will as they affected his visitor.

"I—yes. I don't know. It just seems impossible," was the somewhat incoherent reply.

"Well, well, it's not so difficult as all that." Mr. Jennings spoke indulgently. "You want education, I understand, something better than the village school. Hadn't you talked to Mr. Harding about that?" Peter nodded dumbly. "You thought of College in the future and wanted to work for it; with what aim?" the solicitor went on.

"I want to be a missionary. You can't do that without being able to learn languages and study." The boy spoke clearly enough though he still sounded a little dazed.

"Yes, well, it's all quite clear. Mr. Harding believed in your ability and your sincerity. He spoke to me of you in the highest terms, and he has left you this money which will bring you about nine hundred pounds a year to help you realize your ambition, though even with that you'll still have to work hard, mind you. He has appointed Mrs. Stanhope and myself as trustees of the money and we shall be pleased to help and advise you in every way that we can. The question of where you will live must be gone into, and a good deal more, but Mrs. Stanhope is on the spot and you can talk things over with her as soon as you like."

There were a good many further details to go over, and then Peter found himself in the street once more. His heart was still beating fast, but the gladness which filled it was not so much because of the new possibilities of fulfilling his cherished plans that were opening so wonderfully before him, as the warm comforting sense of his friend's love for and trust in him. The sense of utter loss was strangely lifted. Heaven itself seemed real and near; Richard Harding was there, well and strong, but still interested and caring what happened to him; the Lord Whom he loved and had taught Peter to love was there, but was also here, proving afresh that He would guide and control the life that had been handed over to His keeping. Here he walked into a lamp-post and came to an abrupt halt. An errand boy passing on his bicycle laughed derisively and, rather red in the face, Peter hurried on to catch his bus back to the village. He went straight to Mrs. Stanhope, feeling that after a talk with her he would be better able to explain the situation to his aunt.

A very long talk it proved to be. Audrey Stanhope was able to tell of Mr. Harding's hopes and prayers for Peter in a more personal way than Mr. Jennings had done, and the boy's heart glowed with almost worshipful gratitude as he realized how much his friend had thought and planned for him. He had been anxious that Peter should enter a good school the very next term, and had talked of this in detail in their very last time together, she told him. Mr. Dyer had been interviewed, and his full support promised in trying to obtain a place in the bigger school in the nearby town. He would give necessary references saying Peter was an unusually bright boy, and had excellent prospects of getting a place in a good university. The journey to and fro could, of course, be made every day by bus or bicycle, but Mrs. Stanhope was strongly in favour of finding a Christian family willing to board the boy, and to give him that which he had so far never known, a happy and stable home atmosphere, where he could work for further scholarships without hindrance or petty persecution. Over this last suggestion Peter hesitated.

"It's awfully difficult to know what Aunt Agatha really likes," he explained. "She may be glad to see the last of me, but I could pay her for board and that would make things easier for her. She might want me to stay."

"Yes, I daresay she will," Mrs. Stanhope agreed, "but if it's just a matter of money and she does not give you reasonable comfort and proper food, it's bound to be an enormous hindrance to your work. You must think very seriously of that, Peter."

The boy nodded. "I'll talk to her and try to find out what she really wants," he promised. He could not tell of those little signs of softening he had noticed now and then of late. They were so very small and would mean nothing to an outsider, yet with his years of experience of life with Miss Mason, they meant much to him.

Mrs. Stanhope looked after him with an expression of something like awe when he finally took his departure.

"What his aunt wants," she repeated quietly to herself, "never a word of what *he* wants, and she has treated him worse than a dog all his life. If he has learnt so truly to do good to those that hate him before he's fifteen, he will surely prove a mighty man of God one day."

The talk that followed later that afternoon was by far the longest Peter had ever had with his aunt. Even after he left Mrs. Stanhope he walked about for some time, dreading the moment when such big issues would have to be faced. It was a terrific effort to break down his own reserve, and to steel himself to endure without any sign of resentment the bitter and sarcastic taunts which he felt sure would be called forth, when he disclosed his future plans and hopes.

"I began to think you'd become a millionaire, and gone off to America," was Miss Mason's greeting.

"I'm sorry, I've got a lot to tell you," Peter answered rather nervously.

"Don't you want your dinner?" The question was brusque enough, but it was such an unheard of thing for his aunt to keep a meal for him, that the boy checked the prompt denial that rose to his lips, and though Mrs. Stanhope had insisted on feeding him, substituted, "Yes, please." He resolutely ate the food she had actually kept hot, then, pushing away the plate, plunged directly into the subject with which his mind was filled.

Miss Mason listened in growing astonishment. Her habit of silence served her well on this occasion, but she could not altogether repress a snort of derisive contempt when her nephew spoke of his determination to preach the Gospel where it was not already known. By far the most difficult part was the question of the next immediate step. Peter's face grew red as he sought for the right words to convince his listener of his honest desire to meet her wishes.

"Aunt Agatha," he began after a little pause in which she had still made no comment, "I know you find me a nuisance, and I could go and live somewhere near the school if you would like the chance of being rid of me, but now that I could pay for my keep here, we could be much more comfortable and you wouldn't have to scrape so. You just have to tell me which way you'd like it to be."

Miss Mason stared fixedly at her nephew, her fingers gripped the edge of the table.

"I guess you've made up your mind to get out now that you can," she muttered fiercely.

Peter shook his head. "I haven't," he assured her. "If I thought you'd like me to stay, that's what I'd want to do."

The woman turned her head away. She appeared to be looking out of the window, her mouth was set in a grim line, and no one would have suspected the violence of the struggle that raged within her. Her lips seemed to have forgotten how to form kind or gentle words, and even while she realized with a strange revulsion of feeling that she intensely desired Peter to remain with her, it seemed altogether beyond her power to tell him so; yet she must speak. His new friends would arrange something for him, she had no doubt, and he would be lost to her. She dragged her eyes back to his expectant face.

"I don't see why you should go. You're my nephew, aren't you? Your father left you with me." The actual words were ungracious enough, but behind them there was almost a note of pleading and Peter was quick to detect it.

"All right," he said cheerfully, "we'll settle it that way."

There was no hint that the decision was a sacrifice in either voice or face, though Miss Mason scrutinized him narrowly. She swallowed hard.

"I'll look after you." She brought out the words gruffly, and immediately caught up the empty plates and hurried into the scullery.

The boy looked after her almost incredulously; he realized what a tremendous effort even such a slight conciliation had cost. He was under no delusion that their troubles were over or the victory already won, but he went up the narrow stairs and, kneeling beside his bed, prayed for his aunt with more hope and deeper longing than ever before. Then, in simple and most unorthodox language, he again yielded his life with renewed wonder and thanks to the Saviour, Whom day by day he was learning to prove all loving and all powerful to control his life both within and without, and Whom he could trust entirely for the unknown, untried path which lay ahead.